CW01476732

TERRA'S FATE

TERRA'S FATE

DANIELLE FORREST

The Eternal Scribe Publishing
Indianapolis, IN

The Eternal Scribe Publishing
www.theeternalscribe.com
theternalscribe@gmail.com

Cover Design: Amygdala Designs
Interior Design: Vellum
Printing: IngramSpark/KDP Print

First Edition
Paperback ISBN: 978-1-950795-04-8
Hardcover ISBN: 978-1-950795-05-5
Library of Congress Control Number: 2020906542

PROLOGUE

"*L*et's talk," Kyle Avery said, looking down at the human filth lounging on a cot in the corner of the holding cell. He clenched his fists, jaw tight with frustration and anger.

Springs groaned as Wilhem Haus shifted on his bed, glancing out at Kyle from the deepest shadows. His face dipped in and out of the prison's dim light. It was a dark hole, a cesspit meant only for the foulest criminals.

Then again, what could you expect when you literally betrayed the entire world?

Kyle leaned against the opposite wall, playing at a nonchalance he didn't feel. He had devoted months to finding the culprits, to putting them behind bars. They'd tried to sabotage two separate missions he was on.

Wilhem was the first real lead he'd had. He wouldn't let it go to waste.

So he waited.

From his personal experience, people tended to hate two

1

things: silence and stillness. Kyle excelled at both.

With arms crossed over his chest, he waited. Wilhem lounged as if enjoying a warm day at the beach, soaking up the rays, arms resting behind his head. He'd had little interaction with the criminal at Kennedy Moon Station, but suspected this was par for the course.

His gut churned as he let his mind drift, remembering recent events. The klaxon of an alarm, the red emergency lighting, racing to save their lives, to save everyone's lives. He half smelled the taint of the battlefield—smoke, death, and cordite.

Really, those were the scents of his life.

Time drifted like a lazy river. Kyle stared his prey down. A menacing omen of death that had no qualms or remorse, he did what needed doing, no more and no less.

Kyle didn't check his watch or fidget or otherwise give away his perception of the passage of time. He just stood against the wall like a statue, a deadly harbinger come to punish the prisoner for his crimes.

"I miss him," Wilhem whispered, his gruff voice echoing in the dead air. That voice had seen better days, almost painful in its gravelly, chainsaw tones, and yet so quiet a pin drop could silence it.

Kyle continued in mute stillness, letting the prisoner fill the void.

Wilhem glanced up, his eyes shining from the darkness, broadcasting his pain. "I'm not a bad person." He sat up and stared at his hands in his lap. "Just practical. It was a job." He cleared his throat as his voice got so bad it was barely decipherable. Then he looked up at Kyle, staring him dead in the eyes, a determined strength flooding them.

"It's not over yet."

PART ONE

"There is nothing more frightful than ignorance in action."

— Johann Wolfgang von Goethe

CHAPTER ONE

N *ot so long ago…*

Terra Wilson glared at her computer screen, pen caught between her teeth as the television chirped in the background. She had a vague impression of a debate about shifters, though she couldn't for the life of her figure what the argument was about? What's there to debate? Shifters were dangerous. Everyone knew that.

But shifters weren't her problem now. She just had the TV on for the noise. No, her problem was this stupid job website and that stack of bills taunting her from the entry table in the other room.

It had been months since she'd been "let go." Most of the time, she was lucky to find listings she qualified for, but nobody called her for an interview. It was like living in a vacuum, devoid of all stimuli.

She hated it. She just wanted to work.

Sitting back and sighing in disgust, her mind warped back to that last day, standing in her boss's office, shellshocked as he imploded her world.

"I have to let you go," he'd said, his face deadpan.

"But why?" she'd whined, at a loss for what she'd done wrong to deserve this. It must be a mistake. She could fix this. She had to.

He'd sighed, looking put upon, a spot on his temple throbbing as he leaned back. "You're just not a good fit. I'm sorry."

From the tone of his voice, it had sounded like that was the tip of the iceberg, but he didn't say more.

It still plagued her.

———————

Months had passed since she lost her job. Terra found herself becoming a bit of a hermit. She'd never had many friends, but being short on cash, she didn't have money for midweek lunches and bar crawls. It left her lonely, isolated, stir-crazy even.

As she smoothed her hands over the new suit, one she really couldn't afford, she stared up at the bland, blocky building. Excitement ran through her, causing her hands to shake even as the institutional gray dimmed her eagerness.

Was this what she had to look forward to?

Was this *really* what she wanted?

When she'd answered the call from NASA of all places, she couldn't believe it. NASA! Sure, it was just a secretarial position, but still. It had to be better than the ongoing series of boring office jobs she'd held until now.

But craning her neck up at the painted cement-brick facade and mirrored windows, she wondered. *Is this what I want?*

She shook herself. It didn't matter. It was a job. She reached out, her hand connecting with the surprisingly cold, metal handle as she pulled the door open, her sweaty palm sticking against the surface.

A cold blast of air smacked her in the face. She flinched and froze in place, handle still gripped firmly.

She stepped inside, her muscles stiff from the long drive to the flight academy outside Clark NSS Base where NASA and the NSS trained their pilots side by side.

NASA's outdated red, white, and blue emblem stood out against the gray wall over the receptionist's desk as the receptionist/security guard eyed her suspiciously.

Terra stepped forward, her heels clicking against the cheap sea foam green and white checkered floor tiles. "I'm Terra Wilson. I'm here for an interview," she said as she approached.

He looked down, his closely cropped hair not budging a millimeter as he checked something on his desktop, then nodded. Looking up, he pointed behind her. "Take a seat. They'll be with you shortly."

"Thank you." She turned around, staring at the weird blue sectional as she moved on autopilot.

This is it.

Finally.

Terra sat in the waiting room, the hard plastic chair dimming her high. In her lap, her fingers once again ran over the surface of the envelope. The wording still caused effervescent joy to bubble up inside her.

"I am delighted to offer you the position of staff secretary..."

Her face stretched into a smile and she squirmed in place, her seat groaning under her. She tipped her head up, trying to push down her excitement.

Gotta get through this first.

She'd already submitted her information for the background check. Now, she just needed to pass the drug screening and ID verification. Piece of cake.

Only, she didn't like doctors' offices, and they'd insisted on the base physicians for the testing, which meant another lengthy drive with her nerves jacked up to eleven.

Around her, men and women in uniform sat or stood, looking far more composed than she did. Across from her, a nurse worked behind a clear partition, ignoring the lot of them.

A door opened to her left, just registering out of her periphery. "Terra Wilson?"

She jerked, shifting her gaze to the man in puke green scrubs and dirty white sneakers holding a clipboard. A tired, frustrated expression had settled over his face.

Terra stood, offering him the paperwork NASA had emailed her. He grabbed it and slapped it against his clipboard, beckoning her onward with a jerk of his head.

She slipped past him into a bland hallway filled with government and health posters interspersed with lock boxes next to closed doors.

"Put all your belongings in the box," he said.

She didn't bring much, just her car keys, ID, and paperwork, the couple of items appearing pitiful in the large box.

"Here," he said, handing her a urine cup.

Terra didn't listen as his voice droned on, giving her instructions and restrictions, no doubt. She stepped into the bathroom, closing the door behind her. As she stared at the toilet, relief coursed through her. Thank God her period ended yesterday. She couldn't imagine giving the ornery bastard a cup full of bloody urine.

She smirked. Then again...

She imagined his face bright red and uncomfortable with the blazing proof of normal body functions.

"Hurry it up in there," he barked.

She rushed through her business, handing off the warm cup as she exited.

He jerked his head again, leading her to the next room, where a chair with a single arm rest waited. He smacked the seat. "Up you go."

She did, and he pulled on a pair of gloves, wiping her inner elbow with something cold before palpating her skin, searching for a vein. She flinched as the needle went in, but he didn't even notice.

Can't look.

"All done," he said, pressing a gauze pad to the place where she'd felt the pinch, then smacking a bandaid on it. "Now git."

She jumped up, turning back to him at the door. "When will I hear..."

"How the hell would I know?" he snapped as he removed his gloves.

She flinched then dashed out, glad to be rid of him.

Bastard.

9

Terra sat, watching TV. On screen, personalities debated the pros and cons of treaties with alien races. She had a hard time focusing on it, though, even when the one foamed at the mouth with each comment. Instead, her mind filled with worries and what ifs.

Standing up, she paced her living room, needing to burn off her nervous energy. She shook out her hands, but it did little to relieve the tension. "It's just a stupid job."

Except it wasn't. The months of unemployment loomed behind her, like an unstoppable force trying to bury her. The job market had been a vast, toxic wasteland, devoid of all prospects, all hope. Once the initial excitement had faded, Terra had been almost paralyzed during the interview, even if only for a secretary position. But she'd gotten through it, and now it was down to waiting on background checks, drug testing, and ID verification.

She'd never needed an ID verification before, but government usually required it. Terra wasn't worried. She'd never done drugs, or anything noteworthy, in her life. She'd lived at home, reading books, and volunteering at the local animal shelter because she couldn't afford a pet. Hell, she'd never done anything more radical than sipping wine at a bar with friends.

"There's nothing to worry about. Just relax." She sighed and looked around her little apartment. From here, she could see every room in the place. No curtains covered the windows nor decorations hung on the walls because she still hadn't decided if she wanted to stay. In her bedroom, boxes stacked to the ceiling, and in here, a TV, table, and recliner made up the contents.

How depressing.

A sharp ring sung through the air.

"Coming," Terra grumbled under her breath, "Better not be another evangelist or magazine salesman…"

With economical efficiency, she opened the front door, holding it in place with her right hand. Two stern men in dark suits stood at the doorway, a white panel van at the curb. "Can I help you?"

Dread curdled in her gut.

She opened her mouth to ask another question, but they snapped like vipers, latching onto her biceps in a vise-like grip that hurt. "Hey!"

But they didn't say a word, simply turned around and started toward the van.

"Hey! Stop it. Let me go!" She struggled in earnest, kicking wildly, yanking at her arms to wrench them from the men's hold, even biting at them, but the white, mechanical beast grew ever closer, its maw open to swallow her whole. "No! No, you can't!"

Then the large, boxy vehicle loomed before them. Panic gripped her. Her imagination, never the best of companions, chose this time to pop up an image of her rotting in a ditch somewhere. "No!"

In the next moment, she latched onto the edges of the side opening like a cartoon cat refusing to take a bath. For an interminable moment, Terra held herself on that edge. Tension, panic, and fear kept her frozen. Fate pushed her onward.

She lost her grip, and the door slid closed with a resounding thud.

"No!" she screamed, slamming her closed fists against the contoured metal. "Let me out!" Her throat protested at the abuse, rubbing raw, but she didn't care. Again and again, her fists landed against the door with resounding tones that echoed through her body. Her face burned with emotion as her hands started to hurt.

Then light flooded the interior, and the vehicle rocked with the weight of the two suited men. Terra turned and slammed against the wire mesh separating her from the front seat, but it did no good. "Let me out!"

But the van started up, ignoring her pleas, and jerked into motion, sending her sprawling across the back. Pain twinged her side as she fell on something. It didn't matter. Nothing mattered.

She slid backward, scooting into the farthest, darkest corner. Tears slid down her face, losing control of her emotion as everything else fell out of her grasp.

Why were they doing this to her?

What did they want with her?

The men drove on, and before long, the overpowering emotion faded into numbness, and her brain kicked on again. Terra took a deep breath and re-evaluated her surroundings. They took a turn, and she held onto the wall.

She sat against the back door. Too dark in the windowless enclosure, her hand drifted, feeling out the environment, looking for an out. She put a second hand into the task, brushing her fingertips along the back wall for handles. Didn't vans usually have back doors?

Systematically, her hands ran over every inch, top to bottom. About halfway up the wall, her fingers fell into two holes. She explored the holes, hoping for a latch or lock mechanism, but frustration got the better of her.

With a huff and some hair wringing, Terra shifted back to the side door, hoping maybe they hadn't bothered to lock it. But even she knew a certain level of hysteria drove that hope.

After all, they'd removed the interior rear door handles and installed a screen to separate the front and rear of the vehicle. What were the chances they forgot to lock a door?

Terra held her breath as she reached for the handle which showed up as a dark line against the lighter metal, just enough to tantalize. Just enough to give her a little hope in the dim lighting. She grabbed on, yanking hard, but it wouldn't give.

"Gah!" she cried out as she yanked on it a few more times for good measure, but still nothing. Slumping against the wall, all hope slipped away. A hole opened deep inside her chest, devouring her whole and leaving her ready to cry again.

But this time, the tears didn't come. She stared at the roof above her, a roof she couldn't see anymore than she could see God in heaven. Terra sighed. *God only gives us that which we can handle*, she reminded herself. *I've got this.*

If only she knew what *this* was. Who went around kidnapping people in broad daylight, dumping them into panel vans wearing dark suits? It made no sense. One expected nefarious beings to slink around in the dark of night, skulking in the shadows, but these bastards had been bold as brass. They'd walked up to her apartment like they owned the place and took her away as if it were their God-given right. It made no sense.

Unless…

Her blood ran cold, her heart seizing in her chest. An image from a news program a few weeks ago flitted through her head. In the broadcast, two men in suits had dragged a kid away from his home. The kid had been a shifter.

But she couldn't be a shifter, could she? None of her family were shifters, and everyone knew shifters were a bunch of criminals, stealing and defrauding their way through life, not a conscience among them.

But she'd done nothing wrong. She was innocent. They couldn't do this. She had rights. She was a law abiding US citizen. There must have been a mistake. A mix-up in a lab or something.

Nodding, reassured by that logic, she sat back and waited, certain she would be vindicated once they arrived at their destination, and they would apologize for the inconvenience. Yes, that was what would happen. She just had to be patient.

CHAPTER TWO

*K*yle walked into the task force headquarters, a small conference room on Clark NSS Base. It left much to be desired, but a fire burned in his gut demanding satisfaction. It was early morning and a couple people looked like they hadn't had their daily dose of caffeine yet, their eyes drooping and movements sluggish.

The strong scent of coffee permeated the space, dimming his optimism. He'd never been one to rely on stimulants to get him through the day. He'd served in too many places where coffee was a luxury that just wasn't available.

Kyle stepped farther into the room and dropped into a seat at the long table. As he waited for the first session to start, his fingers worked a steady beat against the table's mystery-material surface. The tap-tap-tap counted down the seconds as more people filed in, taking their seats.

He paused, stilling his hand as he focused on himself. His tense jaw and shoulders telegraphed his inner landscape. He took a slow, deep breath, releasing the tension and keeping the focus there while he waited.

I hate this.

Kyle wasn't accustomed to waiting on others. He usually led the way, giving orders, or ran solo, following each lead to its natural conclusion. Sitting here waiting for the bureaucracy to get their shit together didn't sit well with him. He wanted to *act*, not sit on his ass listening to people debating *how* to act.

Why am I even here?

Kyle frowned, turning his attention to the cheap wood door to his right, but knew he wouldn't budge. He was a soldier through and through. He would follow orders.

And his current orders were to take part in this task force to capture the individuals or group behind the sabotage of the *Orleans* mission. He'd looked forward to taking action, to catching the bastards. It still chapped his hide that he hadn't caught them all while he headed security on that mission. He saw it as a personal failure, one he meant to rectify.

A man at the other end of the room cleared his throat, drawing everyone's gaze. "Thank you. You've been called here to operate in a task force to identify and capture the culprits behind the recent *Orleans* sabotage." He touched a display on the table's surface, and the walls along the long room lit up, showing a slideshow. "*Orleans* Mission Debriefing" was written across the wall in large letters.

The screens changed and the task force leader droned on, Kyle mostly zoning out, his mind processing the information but not needing a recap of events he'd lived personally. He remembered the fighter attacks, the engines exploding, and running through the ship trying to stop the intruders. He remembered interrogating personnel to find who'd betrayed them to their enemies. He remembered rounding up suspected and actual conspirators.

After the slideshow ended, the leader gave out assignments and partnered up field operatives.

"Avery, you're with Kaufman."

He looked up, scanning the room, catching sight of a soldier who vibrated with intensity. Kyle frowned, suspecting he wouldn't like the man.

"That's it. Dismissed," the team leader said, clapping his hands together.

Everyone got sluggishly to their feet. Kaufman made a beeline for him, and Kyle scowled.

"This is gonna be fun," Kaufman said, beaming at him.

Kyle's scowl grew.

Terra yawned as they came to a stop. The long drive nearly lulled her to sleep, and all her nervous energy and panic had long ago melted away.

When the doors opened, she didn't even move. She just blinked as the sudden light pierced her eyes after so long in darkness.

"Move it," one of the men said.

Terra crawled gingerly to the door, the hard metal digging into her knees. As she got close, he grabbed her arm and dragged her out. Not caring when she collapsed to the ground, he started moving before she even got her feet under her.

"Slow down," she said, trying and failing at first to get her footing. After a few false starts, her feet started lagging far enough behind that they no longer folded under her. She pushed up, stood, and finally managed to keep up with the impatient bastard.

Around her, tall fences topped with razor wire stretched into the distance. Green grass served as visual hope with its festive color, but the inner fence and foreboding, dreary block buildings negated that effect. The man not currently pulling at her arm opened a door in front of them. They entered a poorly lit entry room with even poorer decorations and a single desk, staffed by a stern woman. Her face and body language said she'd seen it all and didn't give a shit anymore.

"New one."

"Obviously," the woman behind the desk said, rolling her eyes. "Name?" She looked down at her computer, fingers hovering over the keyboard.

"Terra Anne Wilson."

This is a mistake. Don't they know this is a mistake?

She typed it in, chewing on her lip as she went. "Yup. One sec." Her fingers flew, and she clicked a few times with the mouse, then she pointed at the wall to the right. "Have her stand against the wall, facing this."

Impatient Bastard dragged into place, letting go when her back hit hard against the drywall. Terra grunted in surprise. She glared, but it had no affect. He'd already turned his back, chatting quietly with his compatriot.

"Hey, eyes front," the other woman said, startling Terra.

She looked toward the woman, but with a waggle of the woman's index finger, Terra shifted her line of sight farther left, where the camera lens waited.

Flash.

Her vision went white for a moment. She covered her eyes,

wondering when the afterimages would go away. Clicking resumed as the battle-axe at the desk did whatever they paid her to do.

Terra wanted to ask why she was there, why they'd taken her, but she didn't. No one here would care. No one here would help. No one here would listen.

Patience.

She just needed patience.

They're just doing their jobs.

They don't know any better.

She needed someone in charge, like a caseworker or something. Someone who could review her situation and have it overturned. Clearly, this was a mistake. It should be obvious.

So she stood, back pressed to the wall, feeling like a criminal getting a mug shot, like her life had just flushed down the drain.

And waited.

Terra forced herself not to struggle as two men in uniforms hauled her out of the administration building, bumping her carelessly onto the grass before disappearing behind closed doors once more.

She wheeled around to snap at them, but the door clicked closed, the lock dropping in place with a thunk. Her stomach churned as she looked up at the forbidding edifice.

This isn't over.

She tried to draw comfort from that thought, but it was difficult. Her heart slammed away in her chest, leaving her breathless in panic. She shook herself.

No, this isn't me.

Shakily, she stood, pushing off with her hands against the sharp grass. It did little to reestablish normalcy. What did she know of normalcy? She'd spent the last few months in desperate search of a job, constantly feeling at sea, like the ground was shifting under her feet. Now, she didn't even have that unsteady sensation to ground her. She had nothing.

"It's okay," she reminded herself. "This is just a moment in time. I'll find someone to listen to me. I'll get out of here." She shook her head. "It was just a mistake." But what if she couldn't get anyone to listen? What if she couldn't get them to see their mistake?

Still standing in front of the administration building, she turned to take in the camp. A series of long, one-story cinderblock buildings occupied the opposite side of the yard. To her left, another cinderblock building, square and two-story this time, spat out people at regular intervals. A couple children ran screaming out, the door banging behind them as a woman caught it, easing it closed. A chill ran down Terra's spine as she took in the expression on the woman's face— haunted. In the background, a child wailed, crying out for its mother.

Maybe I'm not the only one they made a mistake with.

She eased across the courtyard between the buildings, uncertain what to do or where to go. She wanted to dash back up to the administration building at her back and bang on the doors until she got someone's attention, but that probably wasn't the best solution.

And what is?

Terra ambled to the two-story building, keeping a close eye on her surroundings, feeling lost. At the edges of her consciousness, she recognized the walls of her cage—chain-link fencing with barbed wire topping it.

I don't belong here.

There had to be someone she could talk to, someone she could convince. But as she surveyed her surroundings, taking in the dozens of men, women, and children wearing drab, gray t-shirts and pants, the unrealness of the situation hit her. How could all these people be shifters? They didn't look like criminals, they just looked like normal people.

She'd always known shifters were devious, but to see this place, it brought that understanding into a different dimension. Chills ran down her spine once again. She could have passed any one of the people here on the street, at the grocery store, at the gas station, and not even batted an eye. How could anyone keep themselves safe with a threat like that?

Clearly, the government isn't doing enough.

Stiffening her shoulders, Terra entered the square building. The doors opened onto a hallway. On the wall, a sign pointed left for "Cafeteria" and right for "Rec Room." No one occupied the hall.

Terra turned right, running her fingers feather light over painted cement blocks in the wall, focusing on the crevices and divots, if only to not focus on other things.

At the end of the hall, a door sat open. Behind it, people milled around, but no one smiled. A couple people sat reading on a threadbare couch. Beside the couch, a bookshelf held a pitiful array of old, worn books and a few games. On the other side of the room, four people occupied a table and chairs, playing cards. No one seemed interested in the game. Children's toys, all worn and depressing, spilled out around an old wood toy chest.

"You're new," a woman said to her left. She walked up to the door where Terra stood, a hesitant smile on her face meant more to reassure than express emotion.

"What is this place?"

The woman gave a knowing, sardonic smile. "It's the land of misfit toys."

Terra gave her a dark look, not in the mood for snark. She needed answers, not attitude.

The woman's face lost all humor. "This is a shifter camp."

Terra bristled, even if she'd already guessed that. "I'm not a shifter."

"Yeah, you are. Every person here has the genes to shift. You're not the only one who had no clue. Most people don't." She rolled her eyes, but the glance back at the sad corner of children playing spoke to deeper emotions.

"They don't?" How could that be? Shifters were dangerous, criminals. Everyone knew that. That's why they needed to be locked up, for the common good.

The other woman shook her head and scoffed. "The government doesn't tell you that little factoid." She looked down, her expression turning sad. "Like you, I didn't have a clue. I went around blissfully ignorant of the ticking time bomb in my own body. My kid tested positive, so they tested both me and my husband. My daughter and I ended up here. My husband is still out there somewhere." She seemed to fold in on herself before speaking again. "My husband's still out there somewhere."

Terra didn't know what to say. What could one say to that? The single sentence held a world of pain, and her mind revolted against the idea. *Not my government,* it said. *Not here. Not America.*

America was the land of the free. How could this happen? But denial reared its head again, and her determination to clear up this obvious misunderstanding came back good and strong. She hadn't expected to meet another like herself here, someone wronged, displaced, but that didn't change the facts. Someone *had* made a mistake. She just needed to get them to see it.

"There are about fifty men and woman, ranging in age from eighteen to sixty-five, plus an additional seventy children, again of varying ages," she droned on.

The statement struck Terra frozen to the spot. "Why so many children?" Her mind again reeled against her views of the world she lived. *Not here. Not* my *America.* It didn't make sense. It defied all logic. Children were innocent, wheren't they? They weren't criminals, not like the adults.

The other woman scowled, but shrugged. "I think some private schools have bowed to parental pressure and started testing students at admission. Nobody wants their kids in a school with shifters." She rolled her eyes. "Nobody considers that *their* child could be the shifter."

Terra opened her mouth, but no words came out. The woman had unfolded a tragedy before her eyes. She couldn't unsee the small children playing in the corner. No part of her could justify that.

"I'm Terra," she said, feeling like the woman had earned that much.

"Oh, sorry. Name's Macey." Macey shook her head. "You'd think I had more manners than that."

"It's okay. Who administers all this?" There had to be someone she could talk with to fix this. The government *lived* on bureaucracy, and even if things moved slowly, if you found the right channels, you could right the wrongs.

"Don't bother. Nobody leaves here. You're gonna have to accept that. You're a shifter. You belong here."

Terra glared at her.

"Oh, don't give me that look. Everyone goes through that phase. First, they're in denial, then they assume someone must have made a mistake. Eventually, there's acceptance, but that's usually a while down the road, and the rest of us have to suffer through all your shit in the meantime. Trust me. Just let it go. You'll be happier in the long run."

Terra turned, not willing to listen. Macey said nothing as she walked away. Retracing her steps, she continued beyond the sign that had directed her to the Rec Room. *I should at least see the cafeteria.* After all, she would need to eat at some point before she gained her freedom.

At the end of the hall, the cafeteria consisted of long tables and benches in parallel lines with a counter at the far wall. The empty room brought home a loneliness she didn't want to feel, didn't want to see. In that room, she saw the predicament of every person here.

But not her. She would *not* stay here. No matter what. She would be free of this place, one way or another. Turning around, Terra walked back to the administration building. She *would* talk to someone, and she *would* straighten this out.

At the door, she paused. She twisted the handle, but it wouldn't budge. Made of glass, she could peer in, but only empty hallway filled the other side. Walking away, she followed the outline of the building, peeking in windows as she went, but each either revealed nothing of value or had shades drawn. When she reached the corner, she turned only to walk face first into wire fencing.

"Well, shit." Terra tried to peek around the fence, but saw nothing but more concrete. "Macey was right."

She collapsed against the fence, the metal protesting with a rattling noise as she fell to her butt, hugging her knees. It didn't matter if some bastard had made a mistake, did it? There was no opportunity for appeal, no court system, no nothing.

How many people like her were trapped in these camps? Terra thought back to every time she'd reacted in fear or felt vindicated when a shifter wound up in custody. She felt betrayed. What had gone wrong with the country that they could steal the lives of innocent people and nobody protested, nobody questioned it?

Except she'd been part of the problem, hadn't she? She'd never questioned it. She'd never protested. Hell, she'd approved, chatting with friends and bemoaning the dangers of shifters and how they should be locked up for the greater good. She laughed, no humor in the noise.

Karma's a bitch, isn't it?

CHAPTER THREE

wo days had passed since they stole Terra from her home. By now, she'd wandered the entire camp, checking out every inch of the surrounding fences for weakness, looking for any opportunity for escape. She found none.

Then again, she wasn't exactly an escape artist. She'd spent her entire career working in office settings. It didn't teach a person many survival skills. Terra could type a hundred words a minute, answer multi-line phones, and use every program in the Office suite like an expert. But ask her to escape a government installation or survive in the wilderness? She didn't know the first place to start.

Now, she almost wished she *were* a shifter. That might have come in handy. She knew almost nothing about them, but she figured a shifter could have escaped this damned place if they wanted.

But what could they *do*? She knew they could wear another person's face, but was that it? Could they do more, like shift into an animal?

She imagined shifting into a bird and flying away from here.

The currents would lift her up, taking her away. The sun would beat down on her feathers and a sharp cry would pierce the air as she screamed her excitement.

But she wasn't a shifter. She was an ordinary person. This was all a big, horrible mistake, and she needed a plan, needed to convince someone, *anyone*, of her innocence.

Or escape. She could always escape.

Terra sighed. She'd spent the morning sitting under a tree, watching life go by. She couldn't think of a better solution, and the longer she sat there, the better the idea seemed. But if she really wanted to escape, she needed to learn the patterns of her prison.

Patterns, then resources. That would be next.

For now, though, she just watched and waited.

And tried not to cry. She'd gotten to where every time she saw a child in here, her chest would tighten up. Then a uniformed man walked through the door of the administration building holding a toddler, the little one clutching him like a vise, screaming and crying for her mother.

Where was her mother? They hadn't separated her from both parents, had they? The idea horrified her.

No one followed. The child continued to scream. The man tried to separate himself from her, but the kid held tighter, pigtails flailing back and forth as he jarred her little body. Finally, he managed to dump her on the ground, then stormed back inside, the little child's cries unable to move him.

Terra jumped up and ran across the distance, sliding on her knees the last couple feet to the child. "Shhh." She picked the kid up, cradling her to her chest and rocking her back and forth. "Shhh. It's okay. I've got you."

The cries continued, but eventually tapered off. First calming to occasional sobs, then hiccups, then sporadic sniffs. Finally quiet, she looked up at Terra with wounded, curious eyes.

Terra hadn't noticed before, but tiny fingers seized her in a clutch that almost pinched. The girl's death grip cut off her air, but she didn't complain. "What's your name? I'm Terra."

She sniffed a couple more times. "Annie."

Terra smiled. "That's my middle name. Terra Anne."

A hesitant smile crossed her face before freezing and starting to fall off again. "Where's Mama?"

"I don't know, Annie. I'm sorry."

The sniffing returned, and her lower lip started to quiver.

Terra held the girl tighter, tucking Annie's head into her neck. "Don't worry, Annie. I'll make sure nothing happens to you."

Annie nodded, buried her face in Terra's neck, and quieted, her hot breath puffing against Terra's skin as she rubbed the toddler's back in long, slow strokes.

Children had a separate bunkhouse, but Annie refused to release Terra, so she'd eaten dinner with Annie glued to her side and paused uncertainly when it came time for bed. She walked down the middle of the women's dorm, military-style bunks lining either side of a central aisle. She approached the opposite end, where an open door waited, through which she could make out a utilitarian bathroom. Tiny showers ran the left wall, while toilet stalls lined the other. Just a couple sinks stood guard around the entrance, and no mirrors covered the plain walls.

"Annie, you have to let go now."

"No!" she moaned, gripping tighter to the soft, gray fabric of Terra's t-shirt, causing the material to dig in painfully.

Terra sighed. "You have to potty and brush your teeth." She probably needed a bath, too, but Terra had no clue how to accomplish that. She remembered always sitting in the bath-tub growing up, but the building only had showers. How was she supposed to give a toddler a shower?

"I don't wanna!" Annie slurred, running the words together.

"It's bedtime." Actually, it was well past the little girl's bedtime, seeing as Terra was ready for bed herself, so Annie should have been asleep hours ago. Terra hefted her up a little higher against her hip and turned to look her in the eye. "You remember what I said when we met?"

She nodded shyly.

"What did I say?"

"That you wouldn't let nothing happen to me," she mumbled into Terra's shoulder.

"That's right. Well, I'll add one more. I won't abandon you. You can go to the bathroom and brush your teeth, but I'm not going anywhere. I'll be here for you. I promise." Terra tilted Annie's chin up, putting a serious face on. "And I never break my promises."

"I see you've made a friend," Macey said, a smile in her voice.

"Shh," Terra responded, not even bothering to open her eyes. Annie lay on her chest, and each movement made her worry that she would wake her. They'd settled down to rest hours ago, but she didn't trust the girl's stillness.

After a shower, Annie had resumed clutching Terra's gray

uniform in a death grip. The shower had been a long, unpleasant endeavor with Annie flailing and shrieking the entire time, leaving Terra soaked to the skin. Terra had changed her clothes then settled on her bed with Annie, but she couldn't sleep.

Quiet breaths, squeaking bed-frames, and the occasional snort or snore broke the silence of the women's dorm. Terra didn't dare to move, though, afraid either the movement itself or the protest of the bed beneath her would rouse the fitfully sleeping Annie.

"How's she doing?"

Terra half-opened one eye, scowling at Macey, haloed by the floodlights peeking through the tiny windows behind her. "Too soon to tell," she whispered. "She's clingy right now, but children are resilient."

Macey nodded. "See you at breakfast."

Terra nodded as Macey walked away, but a surge of panic tightened her chest, leaving her breathless.

Now what?

Terra hefted Annie onto her hip and approached the buffet. "What do you want for breakfast, Annie?"

Annie sucked her thumb, her head tilting as she perused the offerings. "Nana!"

"Okay, what else?"

She pursed her lips.

"How about some eggs?"

The little girl frowned.

"Come on, eggs are good for you."

But her charge didn't respond, choosing to bury her face in Terra's neck again.

"Anything else?"

She shook her head again.

"Okay, I'm going to get you a banana, eggs, and some hash browns, okay?"

Another nod.

Terra paused, biting her lip, realizing she didn't have enough hands. "Well, that summer waitressing had to come in handy sometime." She filled Annie's plate halfway, then another for herself. After only a couple days, she'd resigned herself to the garbage they called food. Still, food was food. She tipped one plate half on top of the other, then slipped her arm underneath, balancing one on her palm and the other on her forearm.

Returning to the table, she swore under her breath. She forgot drinks. Sagging in place, she glanced back at the drink station. The cafeteria had become crowded, the cacophony of human voices playing harmony to the jostling bodies pushing between each other and inanimate objects. She had a new respect for parents worldwide.

"Let's go get something to drink, huh?"

CHAPTER FOUR

*K*yle scowled when his partner beamed at him, a mischievous grin that didn't bode well for anyone. His teeth stood out in stark contrast against his darker skin and an ebullient energy pervaded his large form. Kyle wanted to grab him and hold him back by force, but knew from several weeks' experience that it would do no good.

If Kaufman weren't a fucking fantastic investigator, Kyle would have ditched his ass ages ago. Unfortunately, the bastard was actually useful. He saw patterns in information Kyle could never have hoped to find and picked up minutiae from interviews Kyle often missed.

Kyle excelled in getting people to talk, tracking them down, not studying nuance. He was a sledgehammer. Kaufman was a computer. It meant Kyle always told his partner to stay in the observation room when interrogating someone, but they didn't have that option out in the field.

Unfortunately, Kyle couldn't avoid bringing Kaufman into the field. Today, they needed to talk to personnel from the *Orleans*. They were working their way through a list, going from bunk to bunk at Clark NSS Base.

The stark hallway reminded him of every ship he'd ever served on.

Kaufman walked up to a steel-gray door and banged on it, making Kyle flinch. The door protested with a hollow sound before shuffling started on the other side.

A crack opened at the doorframe, and a groggy eye peeked through. "What do you want?"

"Hi, how ya doing today?" Kaufman bounced, smiling his thousand-watt smile.

Kyle grabbed his bicep, pinching it in warning. Kaufman backed off. "Neil Nussbaum?"

The eye narrowed. "Yeah?"

"You served on the USS *Orleans*, correct?"

"Yeah," he said, dragging out the syllable.

"Tell us what happened," Kaufman jumped in, not able or willing to help himself.

Kyle resisted smacking his forehead. It was going to be a long day.

Something's not right here.

The thought had plagued her for a while now. Terra still hadn't given up hope of escaping or convincing someone to realize their mistake, much to Macey's consternation, but most days, taking care of Annie distracted her.

It had been a couple weeks since Annie entered her life, and on some level, she suspected the little girl had saved her. She kept Terra grounded, giving her focus and purpose when she started falling apart at the seams.

She sat in a chair she'd pulled up to a window in the Rec Room, looking out over the courtyard. Annie sat on the floor playing with toys that had seen better days, but she didn't seem to mind. They still clacked and rang with energetic sounds that grated on the adults in the room. As long as Terra didn't leave, Annie acted as if nothing were wrong.

People meandered across her vision, living as best they could inside these wire fences. In the weeks after her arrival, she'd classified her fellow prisoners into a variety of categories, though she couldn't figure out what differentiated them.

First was filled with people like Macey. Maybe a bit haunted, they'd accepted their fate, but weren't really broken. They were often sad, but they went about their days with a tenacity that reminded her of factory workers in Charles Dickens era stories.

Next contained people like herself. They were the newest. They would rattle the fences, bang on the administration building doors, and yell at the top of their lungs, crying out to be heard, to be saved. She felt embarrassed lumping herself in that category. Looking at it from the outside, it seemed like yelling into the wind—fruitless and an annoyance to everyone around her. Still, the impulse came to her on a regular basis, and she caved to it more often than not.

The last category unnerved her, though. They were the traumatized, the zombies, the broken. They would stare off into the distance, not really seeing you, not really seeing *anything*. They shuffled about, devoid of life, waiting to die.

The thought of becoming one of them terrified her.

"I'm hungry," Annie whined, pulling on Terra's hand.

Terra looked down, smiling at the little imp affectionately. "Well, you're just gonna have to wait. I don't have anything on me."

The girl pouted, then sagged on their joined hands, her legs folding beneath her.

Terra held in a laugh, amused by the counter-productivity of the toddler's impulse. "Do you need me to carry you?" Terra loved her and suspected she had from the moment she set eyes on her three weeks ago.

Annie scowled, standing up once more, then dashing forward, dragging Terra along by her hand. "Let's *go!*"

Terra did laugh this time, but kept to her sedate pace. After all, there was no need to rush. They would get there eventually, and there were far too many hours in the day here at the camp.

Suddenly, a group of men in uniforms spilled out of the administration building. Terra flinched and picked up Annie, holding her to her chest as she hid behind the nearest tree. She watched as the men walked up to a woman in the courtyard and grabbed her by the arms. She screamed, fighting back.

In Terra's arms, Annie cried out in answer to the woman's fear. Terra held the little girl tighter, running a hand over the back of her head. "Shhh."

At the other end of the yard, the men lifted the woman and hauled her off, but she didn't stop struggling. She flailed and kicked, catching one man in the chin. His head snapped backward, but the other caught her wild leg and contained it as they continued inexorably toward the administration building

The door closed behind them and an eerie silence settled over the crowd. No one spoke, no one moved, but all too quickly, the moment ended and people went about their business like nothing had happened.

Did this happen often?

What *had* happened?

Why did they take her?

Terra spotted Macey leaving the women's dorm and called her over. "What was that? Why did they take her? What did she do?"

Macey scowled and stared at the place where the woman had disappeared. She shrugged. "She must have shifted."

Terra was taken aback, her mind slow to click back into gear. The shock she'd felt only a moment ago dissipated, this logical explanation and cause easing that underlying fear of the unknown that had gripped her only moments ago.

She looked back at the doorway they'd retreated through, and guilt tickled the edges of her mind because suddenly it didn't really bother her that they'd taken the woman away. After all, she'd deserved it. You couldn't control your genes, but you could certainly control your actions.

And nothing could make *her* shift. Not in a million years.

———

"Watch me!" Annie said, bouncing in place.

Terra had become a surrogate mother, sort of adopting her. She couldn't believe they'd been here for weeks, that it was approaching a month. Having Annie beside her made it so much easier. "Show me." She leaned over, giving her a smile.

Annie scrunched up her face, making Terra smile even harder, then her blond locks cascaded into a rich red. "I'm like you!" She bounced and giggled, tugging at the two braids Terra had made that morning.

Alarm flew through Terra, and she tucked Annie into her side, hiding the new color from view. "That's great, Annie, but maybe not in public." She looked around, but didn't see anyone. Letting out a sigh, she ruffled Annie's hair. "Now, I want to see your beautiful hair again, okay?"

"Oh-kay," Annie moaned, and the color changed back as easily as rain falling from the sky.

"Good girl." She picked up Annie, bringing her to a spot under one of the few trees, and sat down. "How'd you do that?"

Annie shrugged. "I just did."

Terra frowned, resting her chin on Annie's head, holding her tighter as anxiety swelled inside her, choking her. She tried not to let it show, but feared Annie would sense it. Children were unbelievably intuitive. Her hand rubbing down Annie's back soothed them both, but nothing could silence the implications of what Annie had just done.

Annie knew how to shift. And being a child, she wouldn't have the self-control hide it.

Her heart pounded in her chest, remembering the woman being dragged away only a few days ago. More importantly, she remembered how that same woman had walked like a zombie just this morning as they'd shoved her out into the camp.

What had they done to her? An image popped into her head of two men dragging Annie away as she screamed, "Terra!" over and over again. She flinched, her muscles seizing up, and ducked her head closer.

Not her.

"Promise me you won't do that again in public. Okay, Annie?"

Annie squirmed, separating herself from Terra enough to look up at her with those big, brilliant blue eyes, and said, "Okay, Tewa."

Terra smiled, her heart melting at the mangling of her name. She kissed her on the forehead. "Don't worry. We'll still let you shift, but it has to be a secret, okay?"

Annie nodded. "Okay."

"Good girl."

Terra rocked Annie, her brain running in circles as her mind scrambled to figure out how she could protect her.

Terra sat with her fingers teasing the fabric of her pants as she watched Annie play, the girl's squeals and laughter tinkling through the air. Her mind ran in a repetitive loop.

Annie can shift.

The thought plagued her, haunting her. What could she do? What *would* she do?

She didn't know.

After that little discovery, she'd walked Annie into the Rec Room. Annie kept checking behind her shoulder to make sure Terra hadn't left, which broke her heart a little each time it happened. She had to protect her. She just *had* to. But how? Terra didn't know squat about security, but it seemed airtight here. The dual fences alone would have been enough to keep her in or out under normal circumstances.

But these weren't normal circumstances. She had something to lose, and that made all the difference in the world.

"Well, you look pensive." Macey sat down next to her, raising her eyebrows in question.

"I am."

"I hope you're not trying to figure out how to escape again."

"I am." What other choice did she have? She didn't trust people who could lock away a toddler. She would have to escape, but how?

Macey sighed, shaking her head in Terra's peripheral vision. "I told you already. Give it up. No one's leaving this place."

Terra turned to her. "Well, certainly not with that attitude." Standing, she walked away. She made a beeline for the exit, then the fence, walking along it as she thought.

The administration building was a no-go. It was the only exit she'd seen, but no one left through there. Between the height of the fences and the razor wire, climbing wouldn't do either, especially not with Annie, which left digging or cutting. What tools could cut through fencing? Something strong and sharp, she imagined, but she doubted she could get her hands on anything like that. She would be lucky to find a kitchen knife in this place.

Which left digging, although how she would manage to dig under the fences with no one the wiser, she had no clue. She could dig with her hands, but it would take time. Someone was bound to notice not only the mound of dirt next to the fence, but the dirt on her as well.

Plus, as she walked along the barrier to the outside world, she noticed things on the top of some fence posts that just might be cameras. If they were, this just got a hell of a lot harder.

So, they had to escape in one shot, digging underneath two fences without being seen. Terra came to a point at the corner of one of the buildings used for sleeping quarters. At this spot, the building came within a couple feet of the fence, so close Terra had to squeeze through.

Stepping forward, she entered a mostly enclosed area. The fence arched out to the right, and the three residence buildings hugged together on the left, so close a baseball bat would have trouble getting through. On the fences, nothing that could be cameras waited, and nobody had bothered to install any lighting.

With deep woods beyond the chain link, this area would be pitch black after everyone went to sleep. How long could it take to dig two trenches? Could they get it done by dawn? She didn't know.

But maybe she could use Annie's shifting to their advantage. Could Terra shift to dig faster?

Terra looked down at her hands, the digits shaking as she tried to come to grips with a reality that still wouldn't click in her head. How could she possibly learn, from a child no less, how to shift if she couldn't even bring herself to believe she had the ability?

She didn't know, but she had to try.

CHAPTER FIVE

$\mathcal{T}$erra left the secret space, walking out into the open.

"Tewa!" a little voice cried.

Terra jerked her head up. Annie was running at her, arms outstretched. She tripped and wailed. Terra sped up into a jog and crouched down next to her. "What's wrong, Anna Banana?"

Annie sniffed. "You left." She rubbed her eyes, giving Terra her best pouty lip even after Terra called her by the nickname that always made her smile.

"I didn't leave. I went for a walk." Terra leaned in. "Where do you think I'm gonna go? Do you see any doors? Any gaps in the fence? You're stuck with me. And even if I were to get away, I'm taking you with me. That's a promise. And you remember what I said?"

"You never break your promises."

Terra nodded. "That's right. I don't." She caressed Annie's cheek. "Don't worry, sweetie. I'm not going anywhere. You're gonna be stuck with me when we're both old and wrinkley." She reached down and started tickling Annie's tummy.

The girl squealed, rolling onto her back and giggling so hard she could barely breathe.

"I'm gonna get you, and you're gonna be stuck with me for all time." She leaned over and blew a raspberry on the girl's now-exposed stomach.

The squeals picked up in tempo, followed closely by bubbling laughter that made Terra forget all her troubles.

———————

After Annie'd calmed down from her giggle fest, Terra took her for a walk. Annie gripped her hand like she wanted to squeeze all the blood out of the extremity, but Terra tried to ignore it.

They made their way behind the residence buildings. "Whatcha think, Anna Banana?"

Annie looked up at Terra, her face scrunched up in confusion.

Terra laughed. "It's out of the way. You can do whatever you want back here and no one will see. Completely private."

"Yeah?"

Terra nodded and crouched down to Annie's level. "I want you to be yourself. Always."

Annie's eyes lit up, and she looked around the space with new enthusiasm.

"Do you know what it means to be a shifter, Annie?"

Annie turned back and shook her head.

Terra frowned. "Truth be told, neither do I. How about we

figure it out together? Can you tell me how you changed your hair before?"

Annie frowned, concentrating in a way that made Terra want to hug her. "*I* don't know. I just wanted my hair to look like you and it did."

"That's it?"

Annie nodded and smiled, the expression stretching to encompass her entire face, exposing dimples on each cheek. In the next moment, her hair flowed into a red color to match Terra's.

Terra smirked at the little imp as she bounced away, dancing along. *I wonder what she sees.* "Is it just that simple? Want it and let 'er rip?" Terra closed her eyes, tried to clear her mind, figuring doubts would only prevent her from succeeding. She needed the purity and innocence of a child.

She snorted. Good luck with that. She'd never even figured out the whole mindfulness thing, her mind constantly drifting and thoughts bouncing around like pinballs.

Shaking her head, she started over.

Clear mind.

Picture what I want.

What do I want?

Eyes drifting open, Terra watched Annie run around, trying and failing to do cartwheels. *I want her hair color.* A mental image popped in her mind of the pale blond tresses with little bits of reddish highlights. She opened her eyes but didn't feel any different.

This was stupid.

I'm not a shifter.

I was right all along.

This was all a huge mistake.

I'll never get us out of here.

Annie landed on her butt, legs sprawled out in front of her. A giggle like bell chimes rang out into the air.

Terra laughed, and Annie turned to her.

"Your hair!" Annie jumped up, charging forward. She grabbed a short lock and yanked, pulling it just far enough from Terra's skull to expose the blond.

"Fuck me," Terra said, reaching and touching a strand, then realized what she'd said. "Shit." Eyes going wide, she zeroed in on Annie, but the little girl seemed more interested in Terra's hair than the vulgarities coming out of her mouth.

Thank God.

———

The next day after breakfast, Terra and Annie returned to the little field. Annie ran and played, oblivious to all but being a happy little child.

Terra shook her head. "How does she do it?" After such a short time, Annie had recovered, feeling secure and light of heart. Meanwhile, Terra couldn't go anywhere without heart palpitations. Every moment put them one step closer to discovery. And really, they did seem to run this place like they didn't expect anyone to shift, even though its sole purpose was to house shifters.

Terra stared down at her hand, wondering what more she could try. What was her next step? She'd pulled off the change in hair color yesterday so effortlessly. Disturbingly effortlessly. What if she did it by accident? What if Annie did?

44

The problem was she didn't have a plan. When did she ever? Terra had lost her job and felt lost at sea. She'd ended up spending a month feeling sorry for herself, moping around the house and watching entirely too much TV before she finally started looking for work. She couldn't let that happen this time.

Except she did, didn't she? She'd let herself get absorbed in caring for Annie instead of trying to leave. She'd forgotten her goals, forgotten to gather intel. It didn't matter now.

"How are we going to get out of here?" She looked down at her hands again. The easiest way would be to shift into an animal good at digging. Terra shook her head. "And why not?" She didn't know tons about shifters, but if they could shift into other people, maybe they could shift into other animals.

"God, why didn't I take more biology classes in school?"

All she could remember was a chunky-looking animal with funky claws. Terra tried to visualize that in her mind, imagining her hand morphing into a claw, but it was like there was this disconnect between her brain and shifting. She opened her eyes.

Nothing.

What did I do yesterday? What's different?

Terra chewed her lip, feeling useless.

I am *useless.*

I'll never save us.

I'm not a real shifter.

She shook her head, trying to dislodge the thoughts, wishing she'd spent more time learning meditation. It would have come in handy now.

What the hell did I do differently yesterday?

It had been so easy. She'd pictured her hair, and it just happened, without even feeling it. But not today. Maybe it was her faulty memory. Maybe she just couldn't visualize what she wanted. Maybe she just didn't *want* it enough.

Or maybe I need to just stop second-guessing myself.

But it was *so* hard to see herself as a shifter. It flew against everything she knew about herself, everything society had told her. Terra was a good girl. She obeyed the law, paid her bills, didn't cheat on her taxes, and sped no more than ten miles above the speed limit. She tried to be a good person.

On some level, she just couldn't rectify that notion with her concept of a shifter. In her head, a shifter was a con artist, stealing identities, breaking and entering. Though, now that she thought about it, the things running through her head reminded her of the perception of the Romani throughout history, and most of that was utter bullshit. Maybe this was too?

Even in her head, the question held so much doubt. Except, as she looked around, she couldn't unsee the chain-link fence and utilitarian buildings—the *prison*—set aside for people who had done nothing except *exist*. You didn't need to do anything wrong to come here. You just needed to be born with the wrong genes.

And how is that any different than how the Holocaust started? She didn't know how this would end, but she shivered thinking of it going in that direction. If it did, living in one of the camps, she would be the first to know... intimately.

Terra shook herself, dragging her mind from those dark thoughts, and focused on Annie instead. The girl laughed and played, chatting away as she pulled at the grass around her.

Terra smiled, letting the love she felt for the little girl chase away the toxic thoughts she'd been wallowing in.

Maybe I can do this. For her.

She focused in on that hazy image of an animal's claws. When the thought wasn't clear enough, she closed her eyes, scrunching up her face in focus, forcing herself to concentrate, to think of nothing else. Then, a sensation like things crawling under her skin invaded her, and she gasped, looking down where her hand had stopped in mid-transition. Skin still tan in color, her nails had elongated, the palm a little wider. It didn't look much like she vaguely remembered, but it was something. She looked at her other hand, this time trying to hold the image of her normal hand with her eyes open.

Nothing happened. She scowled and tried not to panic. "Deep breath." Closing her eyes, she tried it again. The crawly feeling returned, and when it stopped, she looked down and laughed, wiggling her fingers experimentally. "It worked."

Checking on Annie, she found her picking weeds and making a bouquet. Terra shook her head. Kids.

She flexed her fingers once more, paying close attention to how each of the joints functioned and moved. Closing her eyes, she let out a slow breath, focusing the image in her mind. The same creeping feeling returned, but she squeezed her eyelids more tightly closed, focusing harder on her goal. The creeping left, followed by a tickling along her skin, which soon left too.

Terra peeked one eye open, letting out a breath of relief when a fully transformed hand sprang out of the end of her arm. She flexed her fingers, a little weirded out when an extra finger off to the side just sat there taking up space. Her arm ended in a furry, wide palm with six short fingers, each with thick nails longer than the fingers themselves. She could move all but the new finger the same as she ordinarily would. The last one, she didn't know how to move. Maybe she'd screwed up. But the big, broad hand *did* look like it would be good at digging. Maybe it would be enough.

"Wow, Tewa!" Annie grabbed her clawed hand, yanking it this way and that and sticking her face inches away from it. "How'd you do that?"

Terra shrugged. "The same way you changed your hair."

Annie's eyes grew big and round.

"But I wouldn't try it. Practice with some simple things like changing your hair and growing or shortening your nails for now. Okay?"

Annie nodded. "Can you dig with that?"

"I don't know, Anna Banana. Why do you ask?"

Annie shrugged. "It looks like a mole hand."

Mole, of course. That was the name of that stupid animal. "Do you want to watch me try with the other one?" She wiggled the fingers of her left hand in the air.

Annie nodded with exuberance, plopping on the ground with legs crossed.

Terra closed her eyes again, pulling the image of the hairy claw with a wide palm, six digits, and long, thick nails. Again, a creeping sensation crawled up her hand that made her want to shake it out, followed by a tickle that soon faded. When it stopped, she opened her eyes and waggled her newly formed hand in front of Annie, who applauded with high-pitched giggles.

Terra looked at her two modified hands, which weren't identical. *It must depend on the accuracy of the image in my head.* Her left hand was wider, but her right hand had longer nails.

"Dig!" Annie said, bouncing in her seat.

"Okay, okay." Terra smiled down at Annie, digging her fingers into the earth experimentally. The dry brown soil under the grass gave easily to her hands. When she tore her hands away, she left a small but significant hole. With another pass, she pulled even more earth away. She laughed. "This is fun."

She put real effort into it, removing great big handfuls of dirt each time. It flew out behind her, Annie cheering her on. When she finally stopped, she'd dug a hole as deep as the length of her arms. She looked up and laughed. Annie had decided to play in the dirt with her. Dirt covered her from head to toe.

Terra wiped a smudge off the girl's cheek, then chuckled and shook her head when her own dirt-covered claws only made it worse. "I'm gonna get us out of here, sweetie."

"Okay," Annie said. She didn't get it, and that was okay too. Better if she never understood this place.

"Let's fill this hole back in."

"Aw," Annie said, tilting her head to the side and sagging.

Terra leaned forward. "If we don't fill it back in, then we can't play again tonight."

"Tonight?"

"How would you like to play in the dark?"

Annie thought about it for maybe a second. "Okay."

"Okay. Let's fill this hole, clean up, and get something to eat."

And tonight, they would be free.

CHAPTER SIX

*I*t was a good idea. Kaufman had come up with it, reminding Kyle just how useful the bastard was. He glared over at the man lounging in a guest chair on the other side of the room, a tablet resting in his lap.

They'd come up empty while interviewing members of the *Orleans* crew. Kaufman had suggested a few people to monitor more closely at the task force meeting a couple days ago. Unfortunately, there was no reason for any of these fuckers to slip up, so Kyle didn't have high hopes of that going anywhere.

But then Kaufman sailed into the office this morning beyond excited, a sardonic grin stretching his face. "Guess what," he'd said, nearly bursting to speak.

Kyle had been exhausted, seriously questioning his aversion to coffee, thinking it was too damn early to deal with his partner. He'd needed at *least* a couple more hours to wake up first. "What?"

"I have an idea for new leads." Kaufman had dropped into one of the guest chairs, looking smug.

Kyle had jerked his head up, grateful for a new lead, a new angle. "What?"

"The fighters."

Kyle had frowned, his mind not connecting with Kaufman's words.

"The men who infiltrated the *Orleans*?" Kaufman had hinted.

"They're dead."

"True," Kaufman had pointed a finger, "but according to the reports, we don't know if they *all* died. We also have their ships and we can gather personal accounts to identify them. Your security team will cooperate?"

Kyle had scoffed. "Of course."

"Good."

It *had* been a good plan. Surveillance footage from the *Orleans* was unreliable at best and eye witness testimony even more so. Still, security personnel were trained to be observant.

Also on their side, sub-space technology and pilots were hard to come by. He supposed, in theory, someone rich enough could get their hands on ships. Or, he shuddered, someone unscrupulous enough could order NSS fighters to attack one of their own. That possibility always left him feeling a bit cold inside.

He stared at his monitor. His office's solitary window sat behind him, making it difficult to view the screen. Through the closed glass, engines rumbled, coming and going from the parking lot it overlooked. Occasionally, he could make out the mumble of voices. It distracted him, making him want to find a quieter place to work, but no place was quiet on a military base.

Tension and frustration gripped him as he squinted at the

display, trying to ignore Kaufman. It *was* a good lead, so why did it feel like the lead was fighting back? The task force started weeks ago. A dozen men and women worked diligently to bring the responsible individuals to justice, and yet where were they?

Nowhere.

Just fucking nowhere.

Terra hunched over her bed where she'd placed Annie for an after dinner nap. Darkness had set in hours ago, and all the women in the building had fallen asleep. Terra had made the excuse that she wanted to read while Annie took a nap. No one questioned it seeing as Annie tended to latch onto her like a leech, leaving Terra little time to herself.

"Wake up, sweetie," she whispered, rocking her gently.

Annie mumbled and curled up tighter into the blankets.

Terra smiled and decided not to bother. She lifted the still sleeping child into her arms. Walking back to the entrance, she was conscious of every breathing body she passed, every soul who could wake up and ruin this for them. She didn't think anyone would stop them from escaping, but no one had to *try* to thwart them. They only had to draw the wrong attention.

She held her breath as she went along, turning her head one way then the other, expecting someone to catch them at any moment. Someone to the left groaned and rolled over. Terra gasped and nearly jumped, then froze in place, waiting for the inevitable. Her heart hammered away in her chest, ready to bolt, but nothing else happened. She let out the breath she'd been holding and took in another, pulling the air slowly through her lips to avoid making a sound.

Not that it mattered. They were all dead to the world, and Terra reached the door without incident. She hefted Annie onto her hip, opened the door, and started rocking her as if trying to get her to sleep. Anyone paying attention would realize Annie had her head resting on Terra's shoulder and wasn't making a peep, but hopefully the ruse would work for anyone watching on video.

She walked around the fence, continuing to bob Annie up and down. Every once in a while, Annie would make a little groan and curl up tighter to her side. When they reached the corner of the building, Terra slipped through and dropped the ruse, dashing out of camera range, then set Annie down, letting her curl up on the ground.

Terra closed her eyes and took a deep breath, pulling up the image of claws once more. The now familiar sensations returned, and she didn't even bother looking when they stopped. After only a couple times shifting, she'd already come to know what to expect, at least with this little transformation.

She kneeled down and dug her fingers into the soft soil next to the fence, pressing her hands down, then ripping them back past her hips. She repeated the action again and again, her hands growing cold with the damp earth surrounding them. Over and over, she displaced the dirt, her hole growing bigger until she had to kneel inside it to go further.

Now, she began alternating hands, curling to the side to avoid her claws as she threw the earth behind her. The hole continued to grow. Once she started going under the fence, it grew more difficult. She had a harder time pulling the dirt away without it refilling the hole or hitting her body instead of going behind.

Mud caked her hands now, matting the fur there. Instead of soft dirt, clumps of mud came up with each pass, the deeper ground saturated. Her progress slowed, but soft, fluffy earth started falling down from the surface on the other side. Through the fence, she could just barely see an ever-increasing hole out of the corner of her eye, which gave her a headache to watch.

After a few more moments, a big fall of soil covered her arms, leaving a gaping hole on the opposite side of the fence. She sat up, shaking out her arms, which had grown sore from the unusual exertion, especially her forearms, which felt ready to snap. *Maybe that's why moles have such short arms...*

Terra patted down the loose soil in the bottom of the hole and leaned under the fence. Yes, she could get under it no problem. Turning away, she rocked Annie again, being less careful this time to be quiet. "Wake up, Annie. It's time to go."

Annie groaned again, but this time she opened her eyes, rubbing them with two tiny little fists.

Terra laughed, because she'd gotten dirt all over Annie in her digging and the girl had spread it across her cheeks in the motion. "Ready to go?"

Annie blinked her eyes, sat up, looked at Terra, and giggled.

"What?" Terra smiled.

"You're covered in dirt."

Terra tilted her head toward the hole she sat in. "I've been playing." She reached toward Annie. "Come on. In you go."

"Where are we going?" Annie said as she awkwardly climbed in, then skittered under and up the other side. When she clambered back out again, mud formed a single skid down the front of her shirt and pants.

"Anywhere," Terra said and followed suit. "Anywhere."

Jackson stood against a tree, hands in his pockets, chewing his lip. He'd come by this monstrosity every day for a week. At times, he'd glimpsed both adults and children walking inside the enclosed areas, separated from the outside world by twin rings of chain-link topped with razor wire. He scoffed. There was something very wrong with a society when it grew suspicious of children.

He'd been tempted more than once to just burn the camp to the ground, but that would leave a lot of innocents in jeopardy. *His* people could never do such a thing. He shook his head. What was wrong with these people?

Best not to think about it. It would only upset him further and accomplish nothing.

"Night would be best." The place seemed minimally staffed, but *did* see the occasional vehicle arriving throughout the day. At night, it became a ghost town, and the spot directly in front of his perch even more so. None of the flood lamps reached that particular point, leaving Jackson and forty feet of fencing in complete darkness.

And based on the wireless scanner he'd brought today, they hadn't even bothered to put up cameras in this location. Around other portions of the compound, his scanner picked up Wi-Fi-connected cameras with motion detection and night vision options. Even if he killed the lights, the cameras would still catch him.

"Could it be a trap?" he said, scratching his chin. It seemed too obvious a gap in the security to be accidental. Yet why would they bother? They couldn't know his people were here.

They were off the grid, nomads mostly. Nobody knew they existed, and they liked it that way. It was safer. You would never find *them* in a bloody concentration camp.

Which was about when a gray-clad figure inside the compound stepped into the shadowed region not covered by light or camera. He could have easily missed him, but the gray of his clothing was just a tad too pale to fade into the darkness. "This is interesting."

The person placed something on the ground, then planted himself near the fence. Jackson could tell he was moving, but not what he was doing.

"What the?"

The man remained there for some time. Jackson just barely made out movement behind him, but couldn't identify it. It seemed to fly through the air, though. As time passed, the man got harder and harder to see, until he disappeared, only his gray satchel on the ground visible in the non-existent light.

"Huh." Then it dawned on him. "He's digging." Jackson laughed. "Clever bastard." And at the rate he was going, the guy would clear both fences in less than half an hour.

The digger popped back out and reached for the gray package. The package moved, then rose. "That's a person." His anger flared again. "A child."

Both disappeared into the hole, then surfaced on the other side. The process repeated on the other fence, and Jackson crept forward. Minutes ticked by as the man again disappeared into his own ditch. Jackson reached the edge of the tree line and waited. He wanted to meet the first person he'd ever heard of to escape the shifter camps.

The two crawled out, then the man picked up the child,

hoisting it onto his hip, and unknowingly walked toward Jackson. While Jackson's eyes were adapted to the darkness, they were almost upon him by the time he saw them clearly.

"You're a woman!"

She screamed.

CHAPTER SEVEN

*J*ackson reacted instantly, covering her mouth and grasping the back of her head before she could pull away. The scream had barely started by the time he acted, and he prayed it would be mistaken for an animal noise. "Quiet. You don't want them to hear us." Her breaths heated his palm, a damp sensation in direct contrast to the cool, dry air around them. She breathed through her nose, the noise impossibly loud in the stillness of night.

She nodded, her hair shifting against his hand with the motion, and he let go. He looked down at the child—a girl if he could judge based on the long, blonde hair—and noticed the woman's animalistic claws. "Clever. Very clever."

"I couldn't leave her in there." Her voice was quiet, hollow.

Jackson blinked, taking a moment to decipher her statement. "You didn't escape for yourself." He saw her in a new light now.

"No." She looked behind her, then turned back to him, her face twisted in worry.

"You're right. We should get out of here. Follow me." He

turned, walking deeper into the woods, but stopped when he couldn't hear her follow. When he looked back, she hadn't moved. She still stood just barely inside the tree line, clutching the little girl in a death grip. The light from the camp back-lit her, casting her in shadows even his shifted vision couldn't quite compensate for. It was almost as if, even after escaping it, the shifter camp continued to create a dark stain on her.

He shook himself, disgusted with his fanciful thoughts. *She's just scared.* He could practically see her muscles shaking. She needed somewhere safe, somewhere *away.* He could provide that. She'd saved herself and a child. The least he could do was bring her to safety.

"Why should I trust you?" she said, breaking him out of his reverie. Her voice quavered, speaking to her emotions.

He reached out a hand, shifting it to match the shape of her own. "Because I'm like you."

———

Terra sighed and hefted Annie a little higher on her hip. After digging under those fences, her forearms burned and felt like jelly, but she figured Annie would just slow her down if she let her travel under her own steam.

She was too tired to be surprised by the man's revelation. It probably didn't help that she could barely see an inch in front of her face. Whatever he'd tried to show her, it had definitely not been a human hand. She'd only caught a glimpse of something wide and stubby.

With nowhere better to go, Terra followed the man blindly into the dark, dark woods. After the second time tripping and nearly doing a face plant, he stopped and scooped Annie up, offering his other hand to Terra to guide her. Annie was so tired, she didn't even make a token protest.

As they ventured deeper into the woods, dark objects and outlines became a great black void. "How can you see anything? There's no light out here."

"We don't need much light to see. I just shifted my eyes to better adapt to the darkness."

"How?"

He stopped and based on the way their joined hands shifted her arm to the side, he'd turned to her. "Some species of animal are much better adapted to the dark than these human forms. Envision the eyes of one of these creatures and you should be fine."

"One of those creatures?" She closed her eyes, even if it wasn't necessary when she couldn't see her own nose, and imagined a wolf's eyes. She imagined the light reflected off the backs, making them shine in the night. When she opened them again, she still couldn't see for shit, but she could make out the outlines of the trees and roots underfoot. She looked to him.

"Good. Are you ready to go on?"

Terra nodded, and he tugged on her hand, continuing to pull her forward. Once she could see, they made quick work, moving through the darkness like wraiths, graceful as wild cats.

Well, he moved like a wild cat. Terra moved like a water buffalo, but she didn't manage to trip after shifting her eyes, which was something at least.

Before long, the light grew shades brighter, and the trees opened up to a dirt road with an SUV parked there. "Get in," he said.

Terra paused, an image of her bloated body rotting in a ditch somewhere floating through her head. "How do I know I can trust you?"

He turned to face her. She could see him much better now. Tall, he stood at least half a foot taller than her, with broad shoulders and features etched in shadow. In the dark, she couldn't tell his hair color or ethnicity. She couldn't even read his expression to gauge his trustworthiness.

He sighed, running fingers through his hair, still holding Annie with the other. "My name is Jackson. I'm a shifter, and I'm not going to harm you. We aren't like the people you're used to dealing with. We look out for each other, protect each other. You're safe with me."

"Okay," she said, and walked up to the passenger side door of the vehicle. "I'm Terra."

Jackson rounded his SUV and opened the back door with one hand. With slow movements, he lowered the little girl to lie on the bench seat. She curled into a ball, oblivious to the world and him. His chest grew tight, a warm emotion washing through him at the sight. The door closed with a barely audible click, and he climbed into the front seat.

The automatic overhead light gave him the first real glimpse of the woman beside him. Terra. Like the kid, dirt and mud caked her everywhere, even her hair, and even in the better lighting, he couldn't tell what color it was.

Against the darker contrast of the smudges, her skin shone through white as milk. She sat uneasily, shoulders still, watching him with suspicion. Still, those gray eyes captivated him. Behind the skepticism lay layers of determination and strength that spoke well of her.

He couldn't imagine what she'd been through. While outcasts, shunned or vilified by the world at large, he'd never been abandoned, never been betrayed by the people he trusted, and he supposed that was how she must feel. He turned away from her and started the car. The sooner they arrived at his people, the better. Nothing he did would make her comfortable or trust him right now.

That would take time.

And he was a very patient man.

They didn't say another word as he started onto the dirt road. Strangely, the silence was both awkward and comfortable. He felt relaxed around her, like he could trust her, even though he knew nothing but her name and that she'd escaped a shifter camp. But he suspected he could grow to like her very much. He saw signs that she held traits he admired a great deal.

Just the fact that she'd rescued the girl said something about her. He didn't know if the child was hers or just a child she'd bonded with at the camp, but it didn't matter. She'd risked not escaping at all rather than leave the girl behind. He didn't hold humans in high regard and didn't believe many of them would do the same. Altruism was a rare trait among their kind, one squashed into submission by their callous ways.

And yet, in spite of all this, he couldn't figure out what to say to her, how to reach her. Occasionally, on straightaways, he would turn toward her, intending to speak, but no words came forth.

But even those moments were short-lived, instantly replaced by a sense of calm and focus. He shifted his attention back to driving. The rest would come with time.

The decision to join Jackson in his car was the hardest decision Terra had ever made. The vehicle loomed in front of her like some dark monster, waiting to devour her, and she was the hapless victim willfully walking to her death. When she climbed in and nothing happened, she took in and let out a calming breath, telling herself que será será. There was no point worrying or freaking herself out over it.

Terra buckled in as Jackson laid Annie on the backseat, and they took off in silence. At first, fear and anxiety overwhelmed her, but no one could maintain that level of stress indefinitely, and she relaxed, turning her curious gaze to her mysterious ally.

She knew nothing about him other than his name and that he was a shifter. He could be a serial killer or a good Samaritan. Uncertainty was a bitch, and as she absently scratched her hand, the sharp claws scraping against the skin, she realized she'd never shifted them back to normal. Looking down, her hands shook, the odd shape, the hair, the claws leaving a queasy feeling in her stomach. Still, she hesitated to shift them back. She would have to close her eyes. While intellectually, she didn't think Jackson would jump on her the moment her eyes were closed, a deeper, more animal part of her resisted showing vulnerability.

The clock on the dash changed from 11:58 to 11:59 before she closed her eyes and concentrated on returning them to normal. *What if I can't do it? What if I screw it up? I'll have useless, mangled hands for eternity.* She shoved the thought ruthlessly aside. *Even if I did mess it up, I could always fix it later, with practice.*

She looked over to Jackson, suspecting he would be more than happy to help her. He seemed like the type that would be a good, patient teacher. She closed her eyes again, took a deep breath and pictured her normal hands. Long fingers, medium length nails—a little uneven from breaking them—and narrower palms. She focused on the feel of them changing back and opened her eyes, smiling at the familiar shape that had returned to them.

They traveled slowly on back roads, mindful of divots and potholes. Jackson would slow further when he turned onto side roads that were much higher or lower. By the time he stopped the car, the clock had reached 12:28. The headlights revealed yet more trees and dirt road. Out in the distance, a glimpse of something white or cream gleamed.

He killed the engine and rotated in his seat, his arm wrapped around his headrest. "Welcome to my home."

Terra looked around and frowned. What home? "Where?" she whispered.

He smiled at her, probably an indulgent expression. "Through the trees there. But I warn you. Don't expect what you might be accustomed to."

"What should I expect?"

He paused, then shrugged. "Home?"

Terra laughed, careful not to wake Annie.

"Come on. It's late. Probably no one's awake, but I can show you around a bit." He popped open the driver side door. Terra held her breath as he reached into the backseat for Annie, afraid he'd wake her, but Annie curled into his side as she often did with Terra.

He came around, opened Terra's door, and offered his hand. "Come on."

Terra grasped it, feeling it for the first time with her own. Warm and big, it gripped her securely, firmly. She gripped him right back and followed him along the path. Around the bend, more cars lined the road, the first a white truck that must have been what she'd seen gleaming earlier.

They continued to walk, and Terra started to flag, counting cars to keep her mind focused. It had been a grueling day, and she just wanted to collapse somewhere soft and pass out.

After she'd counted ten cars, the path opened into a small field containing an entire village of RVs and trailers. Some had tents between them. Billowing cloth and decorations made the place feel alive, wind chimes welcoming them home. Jackson pulled her to a unit on the left, opened the door, which wasn't locked, and ushered her inside.

He led her down the narrow central aisle to the end where a bedroom lay, bed in disarray. "You can sleep here tonight. There's a bathroom there if you want to get cleaned up." He pointed to the left where an accordion door covered a hole in the wall. He set sleeping Annie down on the bed and closed the door behind him without another word.

Terra looked back, a little puzzled at the closed door. Her brain was too tired to even puzzle out why she was puzzled.

CHAPTER EIGHT

*T*erra woke to sun shining down on her head. She dragged the covers up, groaning, unwilling to greet the day just yet. The comforter and big, soft bed swallowed her up, encouraging her to dally.

Then a small hand latched onto her shoulder, pulling at her. "Tewa!"

Terra blinked her eyes open to the dirtiest face she'd ever seen. She laughed. "Hey, sweetie. You need a bath." She touched Annie's nose with a single finger, smearing some caked-on mud.

My God, she's a mess.

She sat up and paused. Instead of the expected cot in bunk-style housing, a tiny bedroom with built in storage surrounded her. She and Annie sat on a wide bed, a vibrant, multi-colored quilt bunched around them. Then Terra remembered last night. Escaping, deciding to go along with Jackson. She didn't really remember this room, but then she'd been half asleep and in the dark at the time.

Oh shit. What the fuck was I thinking?

Her hands bunched the comforter, her jaw locked. *Don't let it show. Don't scare Annie.* She forced her muscles to relax, but her mind still ran in panicked circles. *What was I thinking?* She'd never done anything so stupid in her life.

Why the hell did she get in the car with him? She knew better. That was serial killer stupid. She almost deserved to be turned into a skin suit for that level of stupidity.

But as she inspected the small but neat room, she could admit that at least *this* hadn't ended badly... yet. She wouldn't hold her breath, though. She'd thought she was safe at home and look how well that turned out.

Returning to the task at hand, she glanced at Annie once more. Terra was mostly free of dirt, having taken a shower right before sleep, but Annie had covered herself and the bedding with mud. She went to lift Annie up, but even the act of stretching out her arms hurt. She was definitely paying for the digging she'd done yesterday.

But looking at their surroundings, it was worth it. She reached out to Annie, her arm twitching in protest. "Let's get you a bath."

Jackson woke with a kink in his neck. Not wanting to disturb Terra or make her uncomfortable, he'd slept on the couch. It was too short for him and didn't have linens since everything was in the bedroom, which had seemed the most logical place for them until now.

He got up and stretched, his neck protesting with sharp pain every time he rotated it to the left. He let out a deep breath, focusing on that area, and the tightness and pain receded at about the same time his stomach started growling.

Usually, he would make something up quick and go about his business, mooching a larger meal off one of the older, motherly women later in the morning. They were far better cooks than he, but he figured Terra would be starving when she woke after her adventure last night, and children rarely tolerated waiting for their meals.

Jackson opened the cupboard doors and stared at the offerings.

Terra stepped out of the bathroom to the smell of something burning. She raced across the room, threw the bedroom door open, and froze at the image before her. Jackson stood at a stove, waving wildly at the smoke billowing from something in front of him. She assumed it was a pan, but the smoke was so thick she couldn't tell.

She ran forward, grabbed the pan's handle, only visible once she nearly ran into it, and pushed Jackson out of the way. In one movement, she turned on the water at the sink next to the stove, and held the pan under it. Steam hissed and billowed from it for several moments, but soon the water poured over nothing more than a charred mass and a black pan. She dropped the pan in the sink with a clatter of metal on metal and turned off the water. Smoke continued to sting her eyes, so she turned to the stove, flipping on the fan to pull the smoke away before shutting off the burner.

Terra faced Jackson, but his gaze was elsewhere, drifting down her body. She glanced down and her face turned red. Having nothing clean to wear, she'd rummaged last night and found a large t-shirt, too tired to care. Now, she stood in Jackson's "kitchen" wearing a shirt that barely covered her ass and exposing legs that hadn't seen a razor in weeks because "it wasn't like anyone was gonna see it."

Boy, major mistake. She wanted to race back into the bedroom and slam the door, but she held firm, if a little rigid, in place. She didn't know if fear or sheer stubbornness held her there, and it didn't really matter. It took several moments to work up the guts to look him in the eye, and when she did, she did so with conviction.

Or maybe stubborn determination.

Terra couldn't read his expression. Was he embarrassed? Amused? Upset that she'd borrowed his shirt? Turned on? Or maybe shocked by the quantity of thick, dark red leg hair that made her look like a mutated monkey.

Annie saved them both from the moment of awkwardness with a plaintive, "I'm hungry." She plopped down on the couch with a huff.

Jackson smirked. "Well, I would offer, but you can see what happened the last time I tried to contribute."

"A lot of fast food?"

He shook his head. "You don't generally see our kind eating fast food. We fend for ourselves." He shrugged. "I can cook a few simple things, but sometimes they end in disaster, as you can see. Usually, some of the others cook extra, so I eat there. We all contribute, so it balances out."

Terra nodded. "Why don't you find me a pair of pants, and I'll try to make a meal out of whatever you have around."

"Sure, I'll be right back." He walked away, leaving the RV.

Terra turned to Annie. "Let's see what we've got to work with here." She opened the cabinets as she went, finding small quantities of plates, silverware, bowls, cups—more than adequate for a bachelor who apparently never ate in—along with a single pot and pan and some very basic staples: bread, rice, potatoes. A few bananas and a couple apples sat on the counter. In the refrigerator, she found very little—a few eggs, leftovers in an old Corningware dish, and a few varieties of cheese.

Terra tore a banana off the bunch and handed it to Annie, then started pulling ingredients out of the fridge and cupboards. Except, there was only the one pan… and Jackson had managed to burn it to a crisp. She picked up the pan and scratched at it with her fingernails, but while black char came off, it just revealed more char underneath. There was no way she could clean that before Annie died of hunger.

She grabbed the pot instead. It wouldn't be the first time she'd improvised in the kitchen.

———

Jackson returned with a stack of brightly colored women's garments in hand. Well, actually, they were piled so high he could barely see, but Jemma, their most skilled seamstress, was as generous as she was a busybody. She wouldn't let him leave until he'd spilled whom the clothes were for, where she was from, and how he'd come upon her.

So now he juggled a week's worth of clothes for both Terra and the little girl he still hadn't learned the name of. Jemma had tried to dump more into his arms, but he'd protested. He couldn't even open the door as it was.

Jackson awkwardly cradled the clothes while he reached out to grip the handle. He turned it, conscious of how tilting his arm caused the pile to lean precariously. He had to back away down the steps, pulling the door with him. Then came the rapid shuffle to anchor the door against his body, which almost sent the entire pile tumbling to the floor.

"You should have asked for help," Terra said, catching the door above his head and holding it open.

70

"Thanks." He walked around her, trying not to look down at the long legs peeking out of his shirt.

"You didn't have to get so much." She threw out an arm and stabilized the top of the pile.

He shrugged. "That's Jemma for you." He placed the pile on the entry table, grabbed a skirt and handed it to Terra. "Here."

"Thanks." She waved the material, revealing it, before pulling it on. She motioned at the kitchen table, where the girl sat eating with her fingers. "Grab something to eat. I made plenty, I think."

Jackson looked over at the table. He hadn't noticed it before, but multiple plates stacked high with food sat off to the side. He sat down across from the girl. "So, I didn't get your name last night. I'm Jackson."

"Annie," she said, mumbling the name around a mashed, yellow lump rolling around her mouth. Based on the offerings, it could be any number of things.

Jackson loaded a plate with cheese, scrambled eggs, toast, and an apple and dug in.

Terra sat down at a plate of food with a single bite taken out of a piece of toast. "Annie, you can't just eat banana."

Annie scowled, but snagged a piece of toast and went at it like a lion tearing into its kill.

Terra rolled her eyes, but dug into her own food.

Jackson just watched them, a little mesmerized. For a moment, it was like a tableau of a happy family at the dinner table. He forgot that they probably weren't a family, and the events that had brought them together were not happy ones, certainly not for those two.

When she finished eating, Annie jumped up, saying, "All done," revealing that she too wore one of Jackson's t-shirts.

"Sit down, Anna Banana," Terra said, pressing down on her shoulder.

Annie huffed, dropping like a rock onto the seat.

"You can wait until everyone finishes."

Jackson smiled, memories of his own mother's admonishments, however dim they might be, surfacing briefly, the memories fuzzy with age.

Annie watched the two of them like a predator waiting to pounce. Probably, that was an apt comparison.

When they finished, both Terra and Jackson stood and Annie leapt out of her seat. Jackson reached to the table covered in clothes and chose some children's garments for her. "Here, Annie. What do you think?" He held out a crazy rainbow of colors, an eyesore to most, but he knew children often liked the bright colors.

Her eyes lit up, but she hesitated, looking up at him askingly.

He pushed the clothes toward her. "Go ahead. You can change in the bedroom."

She squealed, grabbed and hugged them to her chest, and raced off. Seconds later, she slammed the door with youthful exuberance.

"She's so adorable," Terra said, turning back to smile at him.

"Yes, she is."

"I still can't believe how well she's bounced back. When she arrived at the camp, she was screaming for her mother, crying and clinging to the man bringing her through the administration building. I tried to comfort her even though I still hadn't come to terms with my own stay there, and for a while, she refused to be separated from me.

"She would latch on, clinging to me, not giving me a moment's peace." She smiled. "That first night, she fell asleep on my chest, still holding on as if her life depended on it. Even though she's away from that place, I fear she'll still panic if I'm not nearby."

"She'll adjust. Children are amazing that way. They can recover from things that would destroy an adult." He sat down again at the table. "So, you sort of adopted her?"

She shrugged and leaned against the back of the couch. "I guess so. I couldn't leave her there. Especially not when she started shifting. I mean, before that, I definitely wanted to escape, but I didn't try in earnest until she came up to me excited to show me her new hair color. Until then, I was just coping. After that, I was afraid."

"You did good. And you'll fit right in around here. You both will."

She gave him a wry smile. "I don't even know where *here* is."

"I guess the best way to describe it would be a shifter caravan."

Terra blinked, a surprised look on her face. "Everyone here are shifters?" She blanched.

He nodded. "Did you think most shifters lived among humans? We aren't human, Terra, even if some can reproduce with them."

"Only some?"

"Women always can. Sometimes men can too if one of their parents was human. But most men in shifter caravans can't. I don't really know why. It just is."

Terra nodded. "What do you do here?"

He smiled at her. The question was just so innocent, so guile-less. "We live. It's a simpler life, but I think it's better. We look out for each other, something humans haven't done for a long time." He scowled, but vanquished the bad mood. He didn't need it.

"That's all a little vague."

"I suppose it is. I can give you a tour and introduce you around once Annie gets changed. If you want, you can also change your shirt. Jemma provided enough for a week or more, so you don't have to wear what you slept in."

Terra nodded, grabbed a shirt from behind him, not even bothering to look at it, and closed herself off in the bedroom with Annie.

CHAPTER NINE

*K*yle rubbed his bare chin, trying to make sense of the information they'd gathered so far. He stood in his office, enjoying the quiet. They'd taped a wall of data with strings and pins to connect everything together.

He couldn't say it made a hell of a lot of sense.

But then, neither did any of the task force meetings he'd been to. Each time he went, he sat back as people argued back and forth, picking apart the evidence, pushing for their own direction in the investigation. Each time, the same thought rolled through his head.

We're falling apart.

As he looked back at the wall, he had to admit the sub-space pilot lead had been a good idea, giving them good leads, but he was still missing something. Unfortunately, two days had gone by and they were running dry again.

He paced along, skirting the corner of the desk which came too close to the wall, but not really taking in the details. He stopped at the far corner by the door, staring at the list of components, passing his finger over the words.

His mind started to click into gear, slowly but it was starting. A hint of an idea, but an idea nonetheless.

A knock cracked against his door, jarring him out of his thoughts. He nearly jumped out of his skin. "What the fuck?" He glared at the door, then sighed.

"Come in."

Kaufman slammed the door open, a huge grin on his face. "How's it going?"

Kyle scowled, irritated with his partner. He tried to retrieve any whispers of the epiphany he'd been on the cusp of, but it had dissipated like smoke in a breeze. "Do you have anything?"

Kaufman's face fell, showing one of his rare moments of somber expression. "No. I checked in with the task force, but frankly," he nodded at the wall, "ours is more detailed than theirs. Any ideas?"

Kyle scoffed and leaned against his desk, crossing his arms. "Just trying to pull something out of my ass, that's all."

Kaufman barked a laugh. "If anyone can do it, you can." After only a second, the serious look returned. "What were you looking at last? Maybe I can give you a fresh set of eyes?"

Kyle pointed at the list. "Be my guest."

Jackson waited for the girls to get changed. A list formed in his head of things he had to do. He had to set up the second bedroom, which usually served as his office. He would be sleeping in there for the foreseeable future. But first, he needed to give Terra and Annie a tour of the caravan, introducing them to everyone.

Then there were his normal duties. He needed to check on their supplies, see if they had everything they needed, balance the books on the caravan's finances…

He sighed.

Terra would need a place among their people. He didn't know what she was good at or what she did for a living before. No doubt, it would be useless here. Most things were, but he was sure she would adapt.

Terra stepped out in a black short-sleeved shirt and vibrant skirt that reached her ankles. Behind her, Annie spun into view, her skirt flying out around her to the music of her giggles.

"Are you two ready for your tour?"

Terra nodded, and Annie latched onto her arm, a shy smile on her face.

They left his home, Jackson several paces ahead, walking backwards, and the girls trailing behind. He couldn't help noticing the distance between him and the girls, and his heart sank. Was she afraid of him? Nervous? She'd been closer in his trailer, but then again, there was no space in the trailer. In there, keeping a distance was a couple inches at times.

"Wow, pretty," Annie said, jumping up to swat at the colorful fabric that served as decoration around the caravan. It was made of thick dyed wool, and served a wide variety of purposes, including acting as shade, a tent, partitions, and wind and rain barriers.

Terra noticed too, but she kept her own council, not even responding to Annie.

He wished he knew what she was thinking.

———

Everything seemed so much *more* in the light of day. Last night, the caravan had been awash in subtle shades of gray, but now the colors assaulted her. Terra fell back a few more steps, overwhelmed after weeks of nothing but gray and a lifetime of her own preference for earthy greens and browns.

Here, they'd unabashedly declared, "We are who we are and the hell with what anyone else thinks." She tended to agree, but she also slowed a bit more with each step.

What am I doing?

As she scanned her surroundings, the thought plagued her. She didn't know what she was doing, but more than that, she didn't know what she *should* be doing. Should she be grabbing Annie and running away again? Should she stay put, gather intel?

Jackson watched her, and again she couldn't read his expression. He almost seemed *more* unreadable now than last night.

I don't belong here.

The feeling only grew as they moved around the caravan. No one else showed their faces, leaving them in a sea of stillness that reminded her of post-apocalyptic movies. Sure, she'd woken up to Jackson burning breakfast, but it wasn't *that* early. The sun still tinted the sky above the trees in vibrant colors, but it had done so for a while now.

The caravan was eerie, quiet and isolating in a way even the camp hadn't been. She felt *other*, different, like a sociologist stepping into a foreign village, invading the culture and tainting it.

I don't belong here.

She listened hard, but couldn't hear anything at first. Then chirping birds and insects serenaded the empty world, sounds she'd rarely experienced living her whole life in cities. Still, no human noises came to her, at least none she could recognize. Had anyone been awake when Jackson left to find clothes for them?

"It's a little early at the moment, but the central resources and storage are up ahead. The community is always set up around them. That's the laundry, that's raw storage, and that's the community hall. Other than that, there's just individual residences."

"What's raw storage?"

"That's where we store raw materials. Wool, shelf-stable food, cloth, and such. Anything that needs refrigeration is stored in the community hall."

"Oh, okay."

Jackson turned to the larger trailer and attached tent he'd called the "community hall." Off to the side, a portable grill/smoker waited to be used, filling the air with the lingering scent of smoke. He pulled back the tent flap, ushering them in. Inside, folding tables and chairs filled the tented space in haphazard fashion. Everything could be moved or folded away for whatever purpose the community had.

They walked through the sea of foldable furniture to the entrance of the trailer. There, it looked to have been gutted. Multiple chest freezers took up the space to the right and bare walls to the left. The entire facing wall was designed for cooking for the masses. Several full-sized refrigerators, three stoves, and plenty of counter space to prepare. The other wall just held straps, probably to store everything while traveling.

"The caravan has lots of meals that start right here. The freezers mostly hold deer meat, but we'll keep frozen bread and vegetables if there's a danger they'll go bad. If you need anything, it will either be here or the raw storage trailer."

Terra nodded as Annie let go of her hand to check out the refrigerator and said, "Where are the bananas?"

"We don't generally store bananas. We don't grow them, so we have to buy them and they don't store well."

Annie pouted, crossing her arms.

"You just ate, Annie," Terra reminded her.

"I like bananas." Her expression didn't pick up at all.

"I know you do."

"Don't worry, Annie. Someone goes shopping at least every few days. We can't produce everything we need. We make a lot of excess to sell so we can buy everything else."

"Jackson, is that you?" a male voice called from behind them.

"In here."

A large man stepped up to the door, shoulders taking up the doorway and making Terra shrink back. He nodded at Terra and winking at Annie. "You gonna be able to help today?"

"Sure. I'm just showing Terra and Annie around."

"Well, it's a pleasure to meet you two ladies. I'm Micah."

"Likewise, Micah." Though friendly, he alarmed her, making her want to run. Without even realizing it, she found herself almost climbing Jackson where before she'd been giving him a wide berth.

Jackson had finished his tour in the community hall which slowly filled as the morning dragged on. There were only a few dozen people in the caravan, and by midmorning, most of them had passed through the tent. As a whole, his people were loud, colorful, and energetic, often leaving him exhausted. Today wasn't so bad.

Terra stayed glued to Jackson's side the rest of the morning with Annie within a finger's distance at any given time. Annie seemed more willing to explore, her eyes wandering wildly, watching everyone with anxiety and awe. She observed the children who ran screaming into the tent with the most intensity, but didn't budge, staying plastered to Terra's leg.

By noon, he'd introduced them to everyone, and he really needed to help Micah with his animals. He looked over at Terra apologetically. "I have some work to do. Do you want to stay here or go back to the trailer?"

Annie looked around but didn't speak. A bunch of children were on the other side of the tent as several women working on various crafts watched. He could see her yearning.

"Back to the trailer should be fine," Terra said, not meeting his eyes.

Jackson nodded, expecting that answer. Terra wasn't comfortable with the people here yet, but she would be in time. He felt confident in that. He would make sure of it.

CHAPTER TEN

*K*yle pulled to a stop a couple blocks away from the warehouse. Outside, wind howled, and cans rattled and loose paper fluttered as the weather beat at them, pushing them across the expanse of pavement. He ducked his head, looking out through the windshield at the property in question. It was nondescript, without any signs or emblems to indicate ownership. In good repair, it was definitely large enough for the suspected purpose, but the entire place was quiet, eerily so.

"You're sure?" He turned to his partner, who dwarfed the sedan's passenger seat. Then again, a supermodel would probably overflow that seat.

Kaufman nodded. "Regular shipments of regulated sub-space engine components, but not among the companies contracted with the NSS or NASA."

Kyle nodded back, but still felt like they were missing something. Maybe it was because this just seemed too damned convenient. It hadn't even been a day or two since Kaufman stared at that list of components and came up with the idea. Shouldn't this warehouse have been harder to find?

"Come on, let's go." He popped the door open, the piece of contoured steel fighting him as the wind caught it and pushed back.

"Well, this is a damned ugly day to be in the field."

He glanced over at Kaufman, who stood behind the passenger door, squinting into the wind. Kyle shrugged. He'd had worse. "Come on." He closed his door, pulling his gun from the holster. The thatched pattern of the grip pressed into his palm, grounding him.

His gut churned as he approached, Kaufman at his side.

Something's not right.

He shook out his left arm, trying to shake off the uneasy feeling. It wasn't helping, and he needed to keep his focus.

The building didn't have windows on the front, just long sheets of corrugated metal and a single door, so they approached quickly, sidling up to opposite sides of the door. He looked at Kaufman.

We should have called for backup.

But it was too late now.

Terra peeked out the window of the trailer, ill at ease after the morning in the community hall. There was something off about this place. She couldn't quite place it, but she had this nagging Stepford Wives impression.

Granted, nobody she'd met was perfect, but everyone was just a bit *too* friendly and accepting, especially of someone they didn't know. It made her nervous. Nobody was that nice without a reason.

Annie bounced onto the couch. "Tewa!"

"What, Annie?"

"I wanna play."

"What do you want to play?"

Annie paused. "I don't know."

"You want to play with the other kids."

"No, I don't."

"You can tell the truth, Annie. It won't hurt my feelings." She changed tack. "What do you think of this place?"

"I don't know." Annie shrugged, her entire body moved by the action.

"Annie…"

The little girl didn't speak at first. She did her adorable "I'm thinking" look where she pursed her lips and looked up at the ceiling.

Terra watched her expressions closely, shifting slowly from contemplative to sad. "You miss your parents, don't you?"

Annie nodded without looking Terra in the eyes.

"Oh, Annie." She pulled the girl onto her lap, holding her close. "I don't know if you can go home." Or if you'd be wanted. How many broadcasts or news articles had she encountered where parents denounced their shifter children saying, "I don't know where it could have come from. It wasn't us."

Annie buried her face in Terra's neck for the first time in days, sniffles assaulting the air.

Terra held her even tighter. "It'll be okay."

Terra had put Annie down for an afternoon nap, leaving her alone with her thoughts. It wasn't a pretty place to be. She considered going for a walk, but the idea of running into anyone sent chills down her spine.

I shouldn't have come here.

But where could she go? Where else was there? She couldn't return to her apartment. Sure, it was on auto-bill pay, and the lease wouldn't end for another few months, but then what? She couldn't get a job. She'd had a hard enough time finding work *before* this whole fiasco. Returning home just delayed the inevitable.

Sitting at Jackson's table, she looked out at the world beyond, seeing nothing but blurs of brown and green. Her nails idly tapped the cheap surface, clicking sharply like a metronome for her mind.

I just want to forget.

Boy, wasn't *that* the. truth. She would have done *anything* to forget everything that had happened. It still felt surreal, like a movie she might have watched once. Things like this didn't happen to people in real life. They just didn't.

This isn't happening.

She shook her head, trying to dispel the weird feeling that had settled there. Children rushed past her window, their voices muted. She smiled, their happy faces tugging at her heart-strings. One looked back, taunting the others, then spun around and shifted, becoming a dog and taking off at even greater speed into the trees. She flinched, looking away, but not before the rest of the group followed suit. She turned back to the packed earth outside as the last of their dark tails, one with a white patch on the tip, disappeared into the woods.

Terra could have done without the reminder. She didn't want to think about shifting. She just wanted everything to go back to normal.

A sick feeling invaded her gut, made worse by the happiness only moments before. It swirled and grew, making her swallow hard. She needed to keep it under control. She breathed slowly through her nose, but it didn't help.

I don't belong here.

I'll never belong here.

Terra bit her lip as, newly revived after her nap, Annie rushed ahead, running down the path leading to the community hall. Once there was a good distance, she would always look back, impatiently urging Terra onward. If that didn't work, she would hurry back, tugging on Terra's hand. It was adorable, if a bit exhausting.

And did nothing to dispel the feeling of exposure as Terra stepped farther away from Jackson's trailer. She wanted to hide, spying on the world with a jaded eye, ready for the next blow. She didn't have that luxury, unfortunately.

Seeing Terra lost in her thoughts, Annie raced back and yanked Terra's hand again, beaming up at her. "Tewa, Tewa. Look what I can do!" She shifted, turning into a little dog, letting off a happy woof.

Terra froze, her heart seizing in her chest. *No.* She dropped to her knees, staring Annie dead in the face. "Shift back." A desperation surged through her.

She can't do that.

It's not safe.

They could never return to the human world, the *real* world, if Annie kept shifting. It would be too dangerous. She wouldn't be able to protect her.

She shook her head as Annie returned to her little girl form and clutched Annie's arms in both hands. "No, Annie. You can't do that. Don't you remember?"

Annie pouted, her entire body sagging. "But everyone else is doing it?"

Terra gave Annie her sternest expression while her heart pounded away. "Just because everyone else does something, doesn't me *you* should."

"Isn't it safe here?" Annie's voice turned quiet, shaky.

Terra sighed, pulling Annie into a hug. "I don't know, Anna Banana. I just don't know."

———

That evening, Terra sat in the trailer, alone with Annie. Jackson hadn't returned yet, and the sun had started setting on the horizon above the trees. On the couch, Annie was nodding off, but still determined to stay awake, to play some more.

"All right, Anna Banana. Time for bed." Terra stood, scooping up the little girl.

"No!" Annie protested, squirming in her arms, but even those protests were half-hearted, not having the energy to be believable.

She dropped Annie onto the bed to start their nightly ritual. Before long, the space grew quiet. Terra sat alone and idle, listless without Annie to occupy her time. She glanced around. What should she do? What was there *to* do?

She glanced at the dirty dishes in the sink, but nixed the idea.

It would make too much noise. A walk across the trailer revealed a bedroom/office on the other end from where they'd slept. The room was tiny and neat, and Terra felt like an intruder just standing in the doorway.

She decided to straighten up their chamber instead. Crossing the trailer, she peeked, but Annie was dead to the world. So long as she wasn't too loud, she wouldn't disturb her. She shouldn't make a lot of noise picking up clothes, and at least she would leave the place as she'd found it. But then she paused, wondering at the wording in her head.

Did she intend to leave? Was she just waiting for her moment again? It would be hard. She doubted Jackson would stop her, but if she did leave, where would she go? She couldn't go back to her old life. That bridge had been burned. Was she just yearning for what she could never get back?

She walked into the bedroom and changed her mind. She needed to do a load of laundry. The sheets from last night were heaped on the floor covered in mud, and she now remembered that hers and Annie's dirty clothes were lying on the bathroom floor.

Terra scooped up the bedding then grabbed the clothes from the bathroom, dumping them together and wrapping them into a ball. She picked them up and dropped them near the door. She thought about walking to the laundry and cleaning them, but anxiety gripped her. Just this afternoon, she'd been walking behind Annie, feeling watched, judged, isolated, and out of place.

Terra stared out the window. Could she slip out and clean them without being seen? But that would mean leaving Annie alone. She looked at the sleeping girl, gnawing her lip in hesitation. She stood there for the longest time, standing on a precipice.

She couldn't keep stalling, waiting in limbo for a solution to smack her in the head. That was how she'd dealt with her problems for weeks now. First firmly believing that if she could only reach out to someone in authority, she could make them see reason. Then allowing herself to get so absorbed in caring for Annie that she didn't do much more than exist, certainly not thinking about the future.

It had to stop. That wasn't any way to live. Terra stared out the window again. Her mind and body danced on an edge, pushing and pushing. She could barely breathe. Like the rest of her, her breath snagged in her lungs, stuck.

On an impulse, she grabbed the door handle, gripping it in a white-knuckled hold, the cold metal pressing almost painfully into her flesh. She closed her eyes, embracing the sensation, the reality of it. It balanced her, centered her, and she took slow, deep breaths.

She glanced back at Annie, sleeping peacefully on the couch, and leaned against the door, hand still firmly on the handle. She smiled and looked away. Somehow, they'd become a family of sorts. And if Terra could get over herself, she felt Annie had a real opportunity to be happy here. That meant more than anything else, didn't it?

For Annie.

She scooped up the bundled laundry, twisted the knob and quietly slipped out. Scanning left and right, no one waited, poised to hit her with a helpful or friendly greeting. She felt certain she would run away from the next person who said, "Hi," to her. She'd grown up in a city. People just didn't greet strangers. It was an unwritten rule.

Terra hefted the bundle over her shoulder and set off, head tilted down to avoid eye contact with anyone she might encounter. Maybe they wouldn't notice her. Maybe they would assume she was just one of the people they'd built a community with.

One could hope.

No one paid her any notice until a small robot, hobbled together with a variety of parts from defunct equipment, maneuvered up next to her and said, "You should twist the cloth before grasping it to get a better grip. You should carry it over your shoulder to better balance the weight load."

"What the fuck?" Terra said, whirling around to face the disturbingly human voice. The deep baritone made her think some tall, burly man had snuck up on her. Instead, she faced a two-foot tall robot, which peered up at her with an innocent look on its face.

Terra backed away, moving toward the laundry, but it followed her, hopeful as a puppy dog.

"I'm Timmy," it said as she stopped.

"Good for you." She picked up her pace, but the little-robot-that-could easily matched her. "Knock it off."

It pouted. It actually pouted. How the hell could it make facial expressions?

Terra sighed. Somehow, the tiny Frankenstein's monster of a robot was almost as adorable as a puppy when it pouted. She about-faced, trying to ignore the thing as she reached the laundry and opened the door, not looking down as it wandered past her.

Two washing machines lined one wall, sitting opposite some counters and shelves loaded with handmade laundry detergent. Terra dropped her bundle on the counter and started loading the nearest washer.

"For maximum efficiency and to reduce the probability of the washing machine going off balance, you should…"

Terra glared at it. "I don't care, Timmy." She finished loading it and added the soap.

"You should use 25% less soap to improve effectiveness and prevent irritation and sensitization."

Terra looked down at Timmy and scowled. She suspected this little monster would be the bane of her existence…

CHAPTER ELEVEN

I should have listened to my gut.

Kyle stood outside a hospital room, hesitant to enter. He should have called in the task force, should have been more cautious. Hell, *he* was the responsible one in the partnership. It was his fault.

He pushed the door open and forced a smile as he entered, his gaze focusing on the occupied hospital bed. A beeping from the monitors serenaded the room and behind him, voices made announcements over the intercom.

"Dude!" Kaufman said, a drugged up smile on his face as his head lolled to the side. "If it takes that much effort, don't bother."

Kyle frowned, scratching at the bandage on the back of his hand. He'd escaped the explosion with minor scrapes and burns. The doctors had shoved him off after only a few hours in the ER. Kaufman, on the other hand, had come in with burns on his back and a punctured lung.

Now, he lay on his stomach, pupils dilated wide as he stared into the distance. Unfortunately, his partner had uneven burn patterns, a combination of second- and third-degree burns that meant he could still feel pain, thus the drugs.

Kyle sat down in a chair next to the bed. "Any news on your prognosis?"

Kaufman shifted, like he wanted to shrug but couldn't. "Just getting touched by lovely ladies on a regular basis. Not so bad."

Kyle scoffed. "About the healing, moron."

"Don't know. Lung is good, but they want to wait and see if I'll need skin grafts or not." He tried to look nonchalant, but the meds left him without any guile.

Kaufman was scared.

It had been a week since the explosion, a week of Kyle filling out reports and attending debriefings. Nobody blamed him, even applauding him for getting his partner out alive, for calling in emergency services. He'd received pats on the back, been called a hero.

Kyle didn't feel like a hero. He felt like a failure, a fraud. He could have done more, *should* have done more. Over the last week, he'd racked his mind, trying to figure what he could have done better, how it could have made a difference.

"Hey," Kaufman said, his voice unusually strong, unslurred. "Don't."

Kyle looked up, surprised at his partner's severe tone. "Kaufman?"

"Not your fault."

"I don't care, Timmy!"

Yep, Terra had been right. Timmy had become the only bad spot in a life that had turned around surprisingly fast. She'd tentatively fallen in love with the culture here. And after a brief acclimation period, she'd accepted the rapid welcome of the community, even if it still weirded her out from time to time. A lot of the women had taken her into their confidences, and the older women had taken her under their wings, trying to teach her new skills or recipes.

She and Annie still slept in the master bedroom while Jackson used his office to sleep in. It had a bed, but was normally tucked away. Terra made meals for the three of them, and Jackson encouraged Terra to take on the administrative tasks of the caravan. She'd been hesitant at first, not feeling she had the right, that someone who'd been there longer, who could more easily be trusted, should do it. She wasn't a member of the caravan, hadn't proven herself, had no real connections to it. What right did she have to take on such an important role?

Jackson'd had a logical answer for every protest. He'd been handling it by himself, and while he managed, it was a lot to keep track of. Eventually, she caved. Not that she minded. She enjoyed retreating into the office and working on paperwork. She often did it when she felt overwhelmed.

"Terra, pay attention," Jackson said, drawing her focus back to the conversation at hand, specifically him trying to teach her to shift.

Terra didn't want to shift. She didn't see where she *had* to. What difference did it make if she didn't? As far as she was concerned, she could go the rest of her life without shifting and it wouldn't change a damned thing. Jackson didn't quite see it that way, so she changed the subject. "It's his fault," she said, pointing at the diminutive robot.

Jackson tried to look stern, but a smile cracked his lips. Behind him, people poured out of the community hall, chatting away.

"Tewa, Tewa, look!" Annie said, running at them at full steam.

Terra searched out the little girl and smiled when she caught sight of her. "Anna Banana!" She opened her arms, then squawked when Annie shifted into a baby wild cat and pounced on her, dropping her to the ground. "Wow, easy on the claws, baby girl." The little cat's claws had dug into her, not doing damage but pinching like a bitch.

Her gut churned as Annie sat up and rubbed her head against the underside of Terra's chin, purring in a ratcheting pattern as she went.

She forced a light tone to her voice. "Now, where did you come up with this one?" Annie had shifted into new and interesting animals every other day. Most times, Terra flinched, unnerved and dismayed by Annie's continued attempts at shifting.

Annie looked around, then shifted back into a little girl. "Caleb showed me pictures of one on his phone."

Terra sighed. Caleb, teenager and tech genius, had designed Timmy the annoying robot, wanting to make an AI that would grow emotional attachment to people. When he wasn't trying to fix Timmy's more colorful character traits, he often showed the children pictures of animals they could try to shift into. Sometimes it worked well. Other times, he had to bring the little one to their parents to soothe until they were calm enough to shift back.

Much to Terra's chagrin, Annie was a genius at shifting, taking to it like breathing air. Terra had no interest in trying in kind, though. She didn't even want Annie to try, but good luck getting a toddler to cooperate when there were big kids doing the same thing not feet away. It was a losing battle. Terra made a motion with her head indicating Jackson should head off, and he smiled at them.

She knew the conversation on shifter lessons wasn't over, but she didn't mind. She had Annie and an entire community to support them, and while they were all shifters, very few of them shifted on a regular basis. When they did, it was often in minor ways, like improving night vision, stamina or coping with body image issues, which were flat out scary in shifters.

A couple people here changed by little bits every day. She had a hard time recognizing them, and she suspected being able to change their appearance so easily just fed whatever syndrome they had.

Terra stood, bringing Annie with her.

"You should lift with your legs and keep your back straight to avoid stress injuries."

She kicked him, sending the little bot flying a couple feet. "Oops, so sorry, Timmy. Didn't see you there. You should be careful where you stand."

Terra smiled. "Hey, Jemma," she said as she entered the community hall.

"Oh, Terra," the other woman said, wiggling in her seat at the other end of the tent.

Terra looked around, but didn't see any sign of Timmy. She'd given him the slip that morning and had every intention of keeping out of sight of him for as long as possible. "Any new projects?"

"Nothing special." Jemma waved at Terra to sit down across

from her. "I've been trying to decide what to do with this beautiful weave."

Terra leaned over the material, soaking up the riot of color. It was beautiful, if not exactly Terra's style. "Does anyone need anything specific?"

"Not really. I mean, the kids always need something new. Hand-me-downs only get so many uses, especially around here." She winked. Jemma had already replaced all the clothes Terra and Annie had been given. Terra helped, mostly by fetching whatever item Jemma wanted. She didn't exactly have a knack for sewing...

"Maybe something salable? What sells well?"

Jemma thought for a moment and nodded before leaning into her work.

Terra felt superfluous and wondered what more she could do. Most of the time, she felt useless, incompetent among these craftspeople. She scanned the tent, but other than Jemma, who was absorbed in her work, precious few were here at the moment.

Terra stood up without saying a word and walked out of the community hall. A stiff wind hit her as she exited and she huddled in on herself until it died. She hadn't noticed it when she entered, but little islands of yellow, orange, and red had pushed in on the verdant leaves surrounding the caravan.

How long had she been here? When did that slight chill hit the air? It felt like only yesterday the weather had been sweltering, oppressively hot, but it was always like that, the weather as changeable as a pregnant woman's mood swings.

Deciding on an action, she rotated on one foot and ambled back to Jackson's office. She felt more comfortable and useful holed up in there anyway. Everyone here was nice, but she still felt like she didn't belong, like an outsider, and that "Stepford Wives" impression had never quite left the back of her mind. Everyone was just too nice, too accepting, and until the dark underbelly showed itself, she wouldn't be able to get comfortable, to relax.

Terra opened the door to the trailer to silence. Annie had asked to spend the day playing with friends, and Jackson was off helping one member or another. She hadn't really paid attention, and she didn't really care.

She sat down at the desk, noting the pile of papers that hadn't existed the day before. Honestly, Jackson could learn a thing or two about organization. She picked them up and placed them in the intake tray.

And froze.

If you asked her what had sparked the moment, she couldn't have said. To this day, she still couldn't figure out what it was, but it hit her like lightning. The other shoe. The dark underbelly. It hit with the force of a Mack truck.

Here she'd been recovering, getting back the optimistic person she'd been before all this happened, trying to find ways of adjusting, and she'd completely spaced. She'd been so focused on the now, on Annie, that she'd blanked out anything else, no matter how critical. Again!

How could I have forgotten?

How could I have been so thoughtless?

So selfish?

Terra stood up, knocking the chair back with a screeching groan that toppled it to the floor. She didn't bother to right it as she jogged out of the trailer. By the time she hit the bottom step, she took off into a flat run, zeroing in on the first citizen she could find.

She didn't know who the leader of the caravan was. He'd been described as old and wise, bringing to mind an old man with a long, gray beard. So far, she hadn't seen anyone matching that description. In fact, not a single soul in the entire caravan looked a day over fifty. But she *did* know Jackson, and she knew damn well he knew about the shifter camp. He'd helped her get away from there, for fuck's sake.

"You," she barked, reaching some poor, unsuspecting person, "Have you seen Jackson?"

He nodded, a nervous expression flashing on his face as he pointed off into the distance. "He's helping do some repairs on a generator. Can't miss him."

Terra didn't dignify it with a response. Jackson had an ass-chewing coming, and she had every intention of delivering.

CHAPTER TWELVE

*J*ackson knelt on the ground in front of the nonfunctional generator. It had been repaired ad infinitum. He very much wanted to scrap it, but they needed it. Caleb hadn't yet come up with the solar generators that would make this piece of junk defunct.

He reached in, adjusted a pressure valve, and pulled his grease-smudged hand out again. "All right, try it again."

The other man yanked, pulling the cord to start it up. The engine puttered before going quiet again. He tried it two more times to the same effect before shaking his head.

Jackson nodded and reached in again, scouring the parts for anything that might indicate why the generator wouldn't start.

"Jackson!" a shrill voice screamed, causing him to jump and scrape his hand against the inside of the generator as he jerked backward.

It took him a moment to realize the voice he'd heard was Terra's. He turned around, surprised by the aggressive expression on her face as she stormed his way. "Yes, Terra?"

She stepped up to him, but didn't speak, dragging in several deep breaths. Anger rolled off her, making him tense up. Finally, she took one deep breath and spoke. "I need to speak with you."

"Go ahead," he said, wondering if he really wanted to hear. He'd lived long enough to know better than to invite a woman's ire.

She glared at the man next to her, who turned tail and ran, smart enough to flee this conversation. "The camp." She didn't say anything else. Just those two words.

"What about it?" He wasn't sure what she was getting at.

Several expressions crossed her face, none of which he could identify. None of them looked good, though. "We just left them there!" She flailed her arms up and down.

"So?" None of the others had the good sense to try to escape. As far as he was concerned, that camp and its inhabitants were nothing more than unfortunate neighbors.

Anger flared again across her face, her body tensing. "What do you mean, 'so'?" She lunged forward as if to hit him, but no blow landed.

He shrugged. "It's none of our business."

Her eyes rounded. "What do you mean 'it's none of our business'? Of course, it's our business. They're shifters too."

He shook his head. "They're a bunch of untrained shifters, raised in a society of fear, anger, and prejudice. They aren't much better than humans." *With unfortunate genes.*

"There are children there." This time her voice turned cold, and Jackson suspected he was about to lose big time.

"Look around you, Terra. *This* is our home, not that camp, not the human world you come from. You're. Not. Human.

101

Stop acting like one. Do you see space for all the people in that camp? We can't support them.

"And then what? Attract the attention of the US government? Do you think they'll ignore us stealing their prisoners? Of course not. They'll hunt us down. Rescuing them puts everyone here at risk."

"You rescued us. You took us in." Terra's voice was quieter now, a sad, unreadable expression on her face.

"That's different."

"Is it?"

He nodded. "You're strong. You escaped on your own. And even though you risked not escaping at all, you brought Annie with you."

Terra stood before him, pensive, relaxing into a blank expression he didn't entirely trust. "I can't believe you, Jackson. You helped me, accepted me, supported me. You gave me food, clothing, and a place to live, to belong. I saw the community here, the acceptance." She shook her head, this odd almost smile on her face. "I knew it was too good to be true. It was. You're not accepting. You're even more prejudiced than the people you shun."

She whipped around, looking back at him before taking off. "I don't care if we can support them here. Anything is better than being imprisoned for nothing more than genes you were born with. If you won't rescue them, I will."

Jackson stood up, reaching out his arm to call her back, but the word lodged in his throat, silenced forever.

Terra dashed away her tears with hands jerky and rigid with

emotion. How could he? Better yet, how did she not see it? What had she missed? She racked her brain, trying to find that one clue, that one puzzle piece that made it all fit.

She threw up her hands. "Why the hell was he waiting outside the camp if he had no intention of rescuing us useless, bigoted shifters, so far inferior to his people?" But she thought she might know, and it spoke worse of him than that entire conversation did.

He saw them *all* as threats.

He'd been scoping out the enemy and stumbled upon her instead. When he judged her and found her worthy, apparently far more worthy than the others he left to their fate, he brought her home.

Terra shook her head, disgusted with him for his attitudes and herself for not seeing it sooner. What had she been thinking?

Clearly, she hadn't been.

And God, the rest suddenly made so much sense now. Why she'd been accepted so readily. It hadn't been generosity or goodness. No, they saw her as one of them, an insider, and not an "other" to be shunned and hated. By escaping, she'd run their gauntlet and come out the other side.

She sighed and kept going, staring down at the packed dirt path, kicking the few leaves that had already fallen. Wind rustled the trees, sending more leaves to flutter to the ground. She walked past Jackson's trailer, not really sure what she was going to do. What could she do? Well, she planned on rescuing the others. That much was certain. But she couldn't risk Annie so she would have to leave her here.

For now.

Annie couldn't stay here in the long run. As soon as she rescued the others, she was collecting Annie and leaving this place. It ripped her guts out even thinking about it, but she couldn't leave Annie to be raised here surrounded by bigots. She would rather uproot the poor girl for the third time in a manner of weeks than do that.

Terra had reached the line of cars before she realized that it had taken them a while to get here by vehicle. She couldn't imagine how long it would take to walk. In front of her, Jackson's black SUV loomed, and Terra had a moment of conscience before reassuring herself it would be fine. After all, she was only borrowing it.

Jackson had sat down on Philippe's front step hours ago. He'd needed his friend's counsel somewhat desperately, but Philippe kept his own schedule, and one could never truly know where the bastard was from moment to moment. He liked to hunt and often returned with a great big buck dragging behind him. Sometimes, he hunted in human form. Most times, he did not.

He also enjoyed fishing. Again sometimes, in human form, most times, not.

Jackson frequently join him, a certain peace settling over him at returning to such a basic, primal part of himself. While this form was his most comfortable, the one he felt most himself in, it helped ease his burdens and stresses to slip free and let out a little aggression on a more worthwhile pursuit.

And it didn't get more worthwhile than feeding the caravan.

"You look like you could use a hunt," his friend said, his deep voice rumbling the words, making him think of the bear form Philippe preferred when fishing.

Jackson glanced up. "Hello, old friend."

Philippe waved the greeting away. "If you don't let it out, it'll fester, and you've already got a hell of a lot festering in that rickety old carcass of yours."

Jackson smirked, shaking his head. "Rickety, huh? You look a hell of a lot more rickety than me."

"This?" He pointed to the wrinkles on his face with his massive paw. "That's just wisdom. It's supposed to accumulate over time. I notice you have precious few."

It was a common joke between the two. Jackson, though much older, preferred the form of a human in his twenties. It felt comfortable to him, right, and Philippe often razzed him for it. Conversely, Philippe wore his age proudly, or at least some of it. He appeared somewhere closer to forty, with fine lines, roughened skin, and little bits of gray speckled throughout his dark hair.

Philippe sat on a stump he used for chopping wood and crossed his arms. Splinters of wood, uncut logs, and bark surrounded him. "Speak."

"I'm not a dog."

"Woof," Philippe said, smiling. "We're men. We're all dogs. And shifters worse than others." He winked.

Jackson looked away, staring at the rough-hewn railing of Philippe's porch, unable to meet his friend's gaze. "Terra took off."

"What'd you do?"

He jerked his head back. "What do you mean?"

"Well, clearly, you did something. Or maybe *didn't* do something."

"Why do you assume it was me? Why couldn't she have been at fault?"

Philippe looked at him, doubt in his eyes. "I've met the woman. Skittish as a mouse, but sweet as can be. She's got a light in her. It's been doused, but all it'll take is a little TLC, and it will be bright enough to light even the darkest night again, I have no doubt."

Jackson grunted, not liking the direction of this conversation all of a sudden. He stared at his trailer, his mind momentarily entertaining the idea of walking away, but he wouldn't, couldn't. Especially not with a friend like Philippe.

"Why did she take off?"

"She was upset that I hadn't rescued the others at the camp."

"And why didn't you?"

"You know why! We can't afford the exposure. And what would we do with them once we saved them? Bring them here? We're self-sustaining here, but not nearly *that* well off. What if the government tracked us back here? What then?"

Philippe shrugged. "Then we leave."

Jackson scoffed. "This is our home. Sure, we don't spend all our time here, but it's still home. Do you really want to put us through the risk of finding a new site for the summers?"

"No, of course not, but it wouldn't be the first time, and it would certainly be worthwhile. Do you honestly think anyone here would begrudge the change if it meant freeing all those people?" Philippe watched him for a few moments, the intense gaze making Jackson nervous. "But that wasn't the entire argument, was it?"

"She said I was prejudiced."

Philippe laughed, nearly falling off his log.

"See," Jackson said, waving his hand at his friend. "It's laughable. I'm not prejudiced."

"Jackson, my friend, you've been prejudiced for decade upon decade. It's only gotten worse with age. Each new experience around humans only reinforced that hatred, blinding you to all the good humanity is capable of."

Jackson's jaw dropped, floored by the words coming out of his friend's mouth. Sure, he wasn't the most accepting person. Leading a community like he did meant having to make the hard decisions, having to be cautious, skeptical. But he made those decisions, and sometimes he made assumptions because he couldn't afford to give someone the chance to hurt his people.

Better safe than sorry.

"I do have to make decisions that may appear that way, but I have no choice," he admitted aloud. "With the camps out there just waiting for one of us to fuck up in public and the general hatred flung at our kind constantly, how can I not? It's the only way to protect our people."

"And yet you can't fight prejudice with prejudice. It only breeds off itself. Besides, I think you have somewhere you need to be, don't you?"

Jackson nodded, uncomfortable with the realization that he might have handled things wrong for too long. He stood up and ran to the cars, ran in the only direction he suspected Terra would go.

CHAPTER THIRTEEN

"*S*he stole my fucking car," Jackson said, flabbergasted by the empty space where his car had been.

A deep laugh roared behind him, and he looked back and glared. Philippe had followed him.

"What do you want?"

"To help," his friend said, holding up a couple bolt cutters in one hand and an airsoft rifle he used to scare away critters in the other. "Though I'm thinking we'll need my truck as well." He glanced back at the green pickup a few cars back.

"What's with the toy gun?"

"Oh, this? Shooting out cameras."

Because why wouldn't you try to shoot out surveillance equipment with a weapon that was only accurate inside the viewing range of the camera… "I'm thinking we won't need it."

Philippe furrowed his brows.

Jackson scrambled for an excuse. "They'd surely come investigate when the camera went down."

"Oh yeah, you're right. Well, no matter. I'll just leave it in the truck." He walked back, opened the door, and tossed it behind the seat.

For all the man was helpful, and Jackson trusted his counsel implicitly, he often had an almost comical innocence about him, not quite seeing through the simpler, less philosophical problems.

"Whatcha standing around for? Get in the truck." Philippe slammed his door.

Jackson shook his head, but jogged forward, eager to be on his way himself.

Terra sat against a tree, using the woods as cover, waiting for nightfall. She'd been there quite a while now and the more she waited, the more the same thought kept drifting through her head.

I should have planned this out better.

She had no idea how she would get in and out without being seen, nor how she would convince and wrangle dozens of men and women to follow her. *I'm not a leader!* But she had to be. For this, she had to lead them, and it was starting to freak her out.

Deep reds and oranges now tinted the sky, and she was no closer to coming up with a plan.

"Do you have a plan?" Jackson said from over her shoulder.

She jumped. How did he know?! How did he *find* her?! "Of course."

He nodded and sat down next to her. "Well, I figured you might need some help. I'm sure you've got a plan, and you can get in and out. You've done it before. But coordinating so many people *will* be easier with a few extra hands."

"Precisely," another deeper voice said behind them.

Terra spun around on her butt, not an easy thing to do, and took in the bearlike beast of a man before her. There was something paternal and warm to him that made her want to like him, to trust him. It warred with the part of her that still felt burned and scarred by the realization about Jackson and the caravan by association.

"I brought the bolt cutters," the bear said, lifting them in both hands, the handles on them as long as her arms.

"Great. Thanks," she whispered.

"I assume your plan is to wait until nightfall? Until it's dark?" Jackson said, drawing her attention.

"Yes. It'll be a lot easier to stay hidden, but I'm not sure how to get the others out undetected. The only gap in the cameras—at least a few weeks ago, I don't know about now is that area behind those buildings. I figure so long as there's no light once night settles in, then there're no cameras. I don't see anything right now, but I could have missed something."

Jackson squinted, turning his head back and forth. "No, I don't see any either. Or any lights for that matter. It doesn't look like they tried to fix their system after your escape."

Terra scoffed, shaking her head. "Classic government red tape."

"Probably."

Terra turned back to the fence a few feet in front of her. She had mixed feelings about Jackson being here. She was grateful for the extra help. At the same time, she resented him not choosing this path on his own. How could he think so much less of these people that he would refuse them the common decency everyone deserved, whether they be people or animals?

It had to mean something that he was here. It just had to. A part of her simply couldn't accept the possibility that she'd been so wrong about him. Then she remembered the argument earlier today and went stiff with rage. "Who's looking after Annie?"

"Oh, Caleb is," Jackson said, before returning to his conversation with the friend he still hadn't introduced to her.

Great. God only knew what she would return to with Caleb watching her. Probably, a baby animal. Hopefully, not anything too dangerous. She looked to the duo behind her. "So, um, you didn't introduce yourself."

Smooth, real smooth.

The other man laughed, not at all insulted by her abrupt and rude observation. "Name's Philippe."

"Terra," she said in reply.

"I know. We may not have been introduced, but I've seen you around and it's easy to learn the name of a new person in a community our size."

"True."

"Well, I'm this knucklehead's best friend."

"Hey!" Jackson protested, not putting much effort into it.

"Aren't you a bit old…" she started but stopped at Philippe's laugh.

"Girlie, you gotta re-align your perceptions. I'm the baby of the two of us."

Terra looked skeptically at Philippe, then at Jackson.

"We're shifters, darling," Philippe said as explanation, which she supposed it was.

"So, you don't age?"

"*We* don't age," he corrected, pointing to include her in the statement. "Not if we don't want to. It's usually instinctual to keep ourselves at whatever condition we're comfortable with."

She frowned at him, not quite buying it. It *did* make sense on one level, except cells still aged. "But you obviously look older than him."

"True, but then, I like this better. I feel more mellowed out this way."

She could see that. Not everyone felt the need to be their best, just look at the number of overweight people in the world. "But then shifters would have been outed ages ago. I mean, I was raised among humans. One of my parents had to be a shifter. Why did they age, but you don't?" It still didn't make sense to her that she was a shifter. She'd shifted before, but a part of her still rejected it, pushing it away.

"Mother."

"What?"

"Most likely, your mother was the shifter. I don't think humans have figured that out yet, but generally only female shifters can reproduce cross-species."

Terra nodded, thinking she might have heard that already. "But why did she age then, if she was a shifter?"

"Because that's what she was comfortable with."

"That doesn't make any sense."

"Well, how comfortable would you be not aging when

everyone around you does? Besides, controlling how you look is a skill, one people raised by humans haven't learned. It's rare for them to shift at all, let alone be good at it."

That silenced her, and she turned away, noting that the sun had set, and while it wasn't dark yet, it was well on its way there. "Maybe another fifteen minutes."

Jackson nodded, shifting in his seat. "Philippe, hand me one of those bolt cutters. We might as well get started. If we're careful, they won't have any chance of seeing us from this side."

"Are you sure that's wise? Is it worth taking the risk? It's just another fifteen minutes." Terra stood, unsure as she looked at the fencing. "Maybe we should wait. Just in case."

"It'll be fine. Look there. That's the closest security camera. With its arc, it won't reach this far. It can't."

"What if it's not whatever model you think it is?"

Jackson smirked at her. "Trust me, I got a *really* good look."

"How? You must have been really close."

Philippe, standing behind Jackson's back, answered by waving his arms around like a bird's wings.

"Never mind."

Jackson crept up to the fence, letting Terra and Philippe come or not as they saw fit. They both followed close behind, Terra nearly bumping into the other man in her unease at starting this before full dark. Really, what would another fifteen minutes have hurt?

Jackson reached the chain link and placed his bolt cutters against the wire, Philippe stepping up beside him to do the same. They made quick work of the task, making a hole big enough for a person to get through one pop—pop—pop at a time.

They crept at speed to the second fence, repeating the process and producing a hole just slightly larger. When they passed through, Terra on their heels, they glanced up at the sky, measuring how much light remained. Terra could still see her fingers in front of her, so she figured still too much. They stood around again, waiting.

Philippe paced the dead space behind the buildings, impatient to get going. After all, who would want to sit around twiddling their thumbs in the middle of a break-in? "What about these windows?" He pointed to the tiny windows high on the walls of the buildings. Big as he was, he could reach it, tapping the glass lightly, making Terra cringe.

"Who could possibly fit through those?"

Philippe looked at the window, then at Terra assessingly.

She didn't like that look. She didn't like it at all. "Whatever it is, no."

"You could fit."

"No, no, I couldn't."

"It would take some shifting, but I'm sure you could do it."

She jabbed her finger at the window a child would have trouble getting through. "How could I possibly fit through that?"

"Shift into a shape that is narrower and taller. Should do it." He nodded, happy with his assessment.

Terra wasn't. She'd refused to even *try* to learn to shift since arriving at the caravan. She had no confidence that she could pull this off, nor did she want to. If they thought it was such a good idea, they should do it. Opening her mouth, she intended to tell them off, but with one good look at them, she closed it again. Each was big and tall already. They would have to shift into a giant to be thin enough. That, at least, she'd managed to glean. When shifting, mass always stayed the same.

She walked up to the window, examining it closer, racking her brain for an image to hold in her mind. Small, but not as small as she'd initially thought. *Think tall. Think tall.*

Moments ticked by without anything happening. She started to second-guess herself.

What am I doing?

This isn't me.

She turned toward the fence, contemplating turning back, walking away. Was Jackson right? Was this none of her business?

She tried to visualize herself as tall and thin, picturing a model from the neck down, one of those anorexic beauty symbols that gave most women complexes. But her mind protested, pulling back, and the creepy-crawly feeling never ran over her skin like it did when she escaped.

"No," she shook her head. "I can't do it." She retreated from the building's back wall.

Jackson stepped forward, reaching out for her shoulder. "Yes, you can."

"No," she hissed, jerking out of his reach. "I'm not *like* you."

"Easy," Philippe said, pulled Jackson back. He stared up at the window. "It wasn't the best plan, anyway. She might have been able to get through, but the people we're trying to rescue couldn't, so it's a moot point."

Terra felt vindicated as she looked at the window, then at the other buildings that served at dormitories for her kind. Her kind. *Her* kind. It didn't seem real, her mind shying away from it, skirting around saying the actual word. But she had to get them out of here. They would have to move in unison. The faster they got everyone through those holes in the fences, the higher the chances of success.

"One challenge to consider—there are more children here than adults. We can probably organize and wrangle the adults easily enough, but the children will prove difficult. They'll either be tired and sluggish, little hellions, or rebellious," she said.

Jackson stepped up to her shoulder. "How many of the children are small enough to fit through the windows?"

"I have no idea. I'm not even sure I saw all the kids. I was told there were about 75 children and 50 adults, but those numbers could have changed." She shook her head again. "This is like one of those nightmare logic puzzles. I suspect most of the children will fit through the window, but what do we do with them while we're collecting the others. The adults would be invaluable keeping track of so many kids. But if we get them first, how do we do it without raising an alarm?" What they needed was a bigger hole.

Terra faced Jackson. "Can we remove the window? Enlarge the hole?" The buildings were made of cinderblocks. "If we break the mortar between the blocks, we can get everyone through the opening."

"That'll make a lot of noise. It might bring security."

Terra stood there, tapping her foot. Too bad they didn't have access to a hardware store. She knew certain types of acids could dissolve mortar, which would certainly be quiet, but they'd already cut the fences. They couldn't risk leaving without the others. "Could we grind it away rather than try to break it?"

"That would take forever."

She turned to Jackson. "We have all night."

CHAPTER FOURTEEN

*J*ackson and Philippe spent the night chiseling away at the wall with shifted fingernails while Terra talked to the adults and older children through the windows, telling them what would happen next. Small noises of distress rose from the open windows, quiet enough only they could hear.

It was slow work, something Jackson wasn't even 100% sure he could accomplish. His arms burned from the steady progress they'd made, but they'd managed to enlarge the holes on the dorms for the children and the women. Terra had ushered women to the children's dorm so that when the time arose, they would be ready to grab kids and flee. She'd offered to help with the windows, but they'd both refused. She could help more by keeping the people as calm as possible. Terra had a big heart, so it came naturally.

Besides, the look in her eye told Jackson her heart wasn't in the offer. She didn't *want* to shift, didn't want to *be* a shifter. He *knew* that, and yet he kept hoping to see a change, a spark that told him he'd been right that first night when he found a strong, clever woman in the woods rescuing a child.

Refocusing on his task, Jackson's hands protested as the last block groaned. The sound of rough stone sliding echoed in the dead silence of the night. He flinched just as he had every time their work had cried out into the dark. They paused, cinderblock in hand, listening for any signs of failure.

Nothing.

They removed the last stone and waved at the men inside. They filed out one by one, their gray outfits standing out against the pitch black. Philippe ushered them toward the children's dorm, where they disappeared. A few minutes later, Terra stepped out and nodded to them.

They were ready.

Terra waved at the occupants of the dormitory, and people ran out in a flood, most carrying small children. Terra vanished from sight as the crowd between them became a solid wall from the buildings to the tree line.

It took too long.

That same thought kept running through his head.

It's taking too long.

We'll get caught.

He didn't even have Terra's reassuring smiles as he couldn't see her. For all he knew, she was gone.

Philippe slammed a hand down on his shoulder, the big bear of a man's version of comfort. The abused shoulder smarted, but he looked up at his friend and nodded.

Time dragged on, insensitive to his state of mind, but finally the last stragglers lurched from the hole, and Terra came into view once more. She slipped into the building, causing him to suck in a breath, before coming back out again with a smile and a thumbs up.

They took off at a run behind the large group, Jackson grabbing her hand as soon as they got close enough. She smiled at him, nerves showing in her brilliant gray eyes.

They ran, the forest swallowing them up, and didn't stop until they reached their vehicles, a dark SUV and a faded green truck sitting side by side.

"We did it," Terra said.

The loud crashing noises of less than graceful shifters dashing through the underbrush serenaded them. Slowly, he registered a dozen people slipping out of the trees around their vehicles, waiting for direction, orders.

Relief flooded him that not all those they'd freed had sought them out, looking for guidance, but a dozen still stretched their numbers greatly. How the heck would they find room for the lot?

"Macey!" Terra jogged up to a woman.

Macey shook her head. "I thought I told you no one gets out of there."

"Yeah, not with that attitude." Terra smiled, maybe at an inside joke because Macey smiled too, her face stiff, like she'd forgotten how.

"Well, everyone, let's go. It's gonna be a tight fit," Jackson said as he waved them to the vehicles. A lot of people would be taking a ride in the truck bed.

Terra sat on Philippe's front stoop as the first flush of dawn tinted the sky, looking out at the new "tent" they'd set up at the edge of the caravan. No one had space for twelve extra people, so it was the best they could do at the moment. Macey and her daughter were staying with Philippe in the trailer behind them. The two had protested as there was only one bed in the tiny trailer, but Philippe had insisted, stating, "I can sleep anywhere." Terra couldn't help imagining him as a bear and tended to agree.

"We shouldn't stay here," Jackson said, cutting into Terra's inner world.

She had to admit, being so close to the camp had given her the creeps at times, but she didn't see any other way. Was there somewhere else for the group to go?

"The season's not over," Philippe cut in from his spot on a log in the yard. "We'd leave crops unharvested, and correct me if I'm wrong, but isn't the other site usually rented out this time of year?"

Terra blinked and resisted smacking her forehead. She was an idiot. She'd been managing all the paperwork and finances for the caravan. She'd wondered about the rental agreements and AirBNB, but she hadn't thought anything of it. She chided herself now for not figuring it out. After all, it was a caravan. Caravans migrate. "There's a rental agreement through the end of the month, but the AirBNB account is shut down after that."

Jackson scowled, not liking that answer.

"Where else can we go?"

Jackson scoffed. "You know? Once upon a time, we could go wherever we wanted. Now, finding somewhere large enough to settle an entire caravan is like pulling teeth. You can't just park it anywhere. People will call the police, tow you, even arrest you. I don't know what the world's coming to."

Terra smirked. She'd never noticed before, but Jackson was a lot older than he appeared.

"There's nowhere to go, Jackson," Philippe said, his voice calm, soothing.

"I can look into rental spots, places we can reserve last minute that'll fit us. It's not ideal, but it gives us an option. We should be prepared to leave at the drop of a hat. We should also have someone monitoring the camp, watching for any signs they might search the area, might find us."

Jackson nodded and stood. "I'll get someone on the recon. Terra, find us a place."

Terra returned the gesture and headed back to the office. Looked like they had a plan.

———

Over the next few weeks, they stayed on high alert. Terra didn't notice whoever happened to be on surveillance at any given moment, but tension thickened the air, keeping everyone on edge. She wanted to forget about it. After all, this level of stress didn't help anyone. But her mind kept wandering back to that little plot in the mountains she'd found.

Some people adapted readily to their new environment. The children, as always, had it the easiest. They thrived on meeting new people and the colorful clothes Jemma handed out like candy. Beth, Macey's daughter, handled it worst of all the kids. She didn't interact with the others her age, and she drew even further inward when she watched men playing with children. Did she miss her father?

Terra knew that Macey missed her husband. Of the adults from the camp, she adapted the poorest as well. A female construction worker and male carpenter managed the transition best. None of them trusted easily, but most felt more secure when they could contribute meaningfully to the group, feeling they were earning their keep.

But every day, Macey only grew worse, not better. At first, Macey had been happy to see Terra, and she'd watched as a weight lifted off Macey's shoulders. But little by little, a cloud settled over Macey's mind. She tried for Beth's sake, but either Beth could read her mother's mood, or they were simply in the same state, each feeding off the other.

She sat on the steps of Jackson's trailer, staring at Philippe's shiny silver bullet. She couldn't imagine even two people living in the thing, but then she'd been surprised by how comfortably she and Annie had managed in their new home.

In the distance, children giggled and squealed, a constant sound here at the caravan. It was a jarring, but welcome, contrast to her old life, more apt to hear yelling, car horns, slamming doors, and thumping music than happiness of any kind.

Her hand rested on the wood step, picking at splinters as she thought.

What could she *do?* She felt she needed to do *something*, but what? Macey and Beth hadn't left the trailer today, even though it was past noon. Based on the size, she couldn't imagine keeping a child cooped up in there comfortably, which meant they were probably lazing about, wallowing in their individual miseries.

What would happen if they were left like that?

Terra didn't want to know.

CHAPTER FIFTEEN

*K*yle sat, frowning at the phone.

What the fuck?

He'd just returned from the hospital again. Kaufman had been in recovery for weeks now. This time, he stepped into his office only to receive a call from his duty officer.

"You've been removed from the task force," she'd said, her stern military mien even more abrasive over the phone. He'd drank with the woman before when off duty, so it was always a bit jarring when she pulled on her military mask, changing from an energetic, positive person to a badass who'd just as soon bite your ass off as look at you. She was so laid back when off duty, almost a pushover, but she would lay you out if you tried anything.

The words still rung through his head.

You've been removed from the task force.

Why? He didn't understand. The conversation had been short, just those words and a statement he would be contacted with further instructions.

Was he in trouble after all for the explosion? Was he about to be punished?

He swiveled his chair, staring out the window, but not really seeing anything. The air conditioner kicked on, whirring to life. Details filtered into his brain.

Metal window frame.

Dirty blinds.

Reflections in glass.

He let the details blur and settle into nothingness until the phone ringing jarred him out of his reverie. He spun around, snatching it up.

"Avery," he barked into the phone.

"How are things on your end?" Tristan drawled.

Kyle sneered, a slight edge in his voice. "Captain Faulk. Somehow, I have a feeling you're to blame for the call I just received from my duty officer."

" 'Fraid so. I've got a mission for you. Meet me in my office at nine."

Kyle sat up straight, intrigued. "See you then."

"Jackson," Terra said in a sing-song voice, slipping up behind him as he went about making the colorful tent a little more fit for its residents. It was dark inside the tent, even with the main flap open to let in light. A large, open enclosure, it provided little privacy, with pillows and blankets that served as sleeping bags on the dirt floor. It wasn't ideal and with the weather threatening to change, would not do for long. They still had a week before they could move.

Jackson kept frowning down at the area, like it offended him. She'd come to realize he took his role very seriously. He felt compelled to take care of those in his charge, and these new people from the camp were definitely in his charge.

Whether he liked it or not.

He sighed and turned around. "What is it, Terra?"

"I'd like to take Macey to see her husband. I know she missed him while at the camp. I think it's worse now."

Jackson shook his head. "That's a bad idea."

Terra fidgeted in place but held her ground. "She needs closure. Maybe it'll be a happy reunion, maybe it'll be a train wreck, but I don't think she can move on until she gets that."

"And what if she wants to stay with her husband?" Jackson spread his arms wide. "They can't exactly go about their normal life, now can they?"

"They can stay here."

"Oh, no." He shook his head. "There are no humans here, and I intend to keep it that way."

"Jackson!"

"No."

"You're such a fucking bigot."

"I'm not, and I said no. That's final."

Terra scowled. This wasn't over.

———

"I don't know how you talked me into this," Jackson said, glaring at the building across the street, his arms crossed as he sat in the driver's seat. The building *screamed* human, with its quaint, well-manicured lawn, well-trimmed bushes, and perfectly coordinated paint job. Everything was clean, everything was quiet.

It gave him the creeps.

On the radio, a talk show debated back and forth about the mixed feelings in the populace regarding the Incirrina and the treaty mission to the Kennedy Moon Station. Some chimed in with how great it was, that it would bring Earth into a new era, that it would make the world safer to have allies on other planets. But for every caller insisting it was good, another called spouting hate, that the Incirrina were freaks, monsters, that they would turn on us. They asked how we could trust creatures that had nothing in common with us, no common history, no common experiences.

And it only got worse from there.

Jackson grumbled about it not being any of their business, turned off the radio, and glared out the window again. Just as well, Terra had grown increasingly agitated with each minute they listened to that garbage.

He didn't like seeing her like that, but wondered why it upset her so. Did it remind her of her own prejudices? Or did it remind her of being taken away? He somehow didn't see her as being terribly introspective. She seemed to focus more on the problems of others.

Case in point: driving God only knew how long to sit outside a human's house so that her friend, Macey, could get closure.

He couldn't believe he'd agreed to this, but Terra had been persistent, like a terrier latching on even though their feet had long left the ground. It didn't even take twenty-four hours for him to fold. Bundling the three of them in his SUV, he'd driven off into the human world, a place he'd never wanted to visit.

He just wanted to get back home.

———————

Macey ran her sweaty palms over her pants, rubbing them over and over, afraid to knock on the door, afraid of the unknown. Had he missed her? Had he mourned her? Had he looked for her? She didn't know, and it ate away at her insides.

She checked the driveway, confirming yet again that he was home. A big, silver electric SUV sat on the pavement, waiting on its owner's pleasure. It was the same car, the same car they'd driven out on date nights, the same car she'd watched take off every morning when he left for work. But she wasn't the same, and she very much doubted he was either. Could they find their way back to each other? A nagging feeling in her gut said no.

She hated her gut right about now.

Macey could feel the caravan leader's stare, egging her on, demanding she get on with it. It only made her more nervous. She turned around, and yep, his glare practically melted her to the brick steps. She didn't like him. There was something wrong with him. But Terra was a friend, and her friend seemed to like him, so she would let those feelings go as best she could.

She and Terra didn't see eye to eye, but the woman had an inner strength she couldn't fathom, let alone experience herself. Macey had adapted, accepted. Terra had rebelled, fought, fled. Where Macey had given up, Terra had searched for an out, for a solution, and she'd succeeded. It made Macey feel small, weak, and in awe of the other woman.

She needed to channel a bit of Terra right now. Terra wouldn't stand here on this doorstep pondering her naval lint.

She would charge up to the door and bang on it like there was no tomorrow.

Macey lifted her hand, hovering over the painted wood. Another moment passed. She wondered if she was doing the right thing, but then she thought of her daughter. She'd become a ghost, not even recognizable as the happy little girl she'd been before they'd received those terrible test results. Macey raised her chin and knocked. Moments later, footsteps rang out on the hardwood floors, and Macey held her breath.

This was it.

The door opened, and she smiled. He looked so handsome, his hair tousled and his eyes sleepy, like he still hadn't had his morning coffee. That perfect moment didn't last, though. Recognition crossed his face, and hope surged through her.

Only to get crushed a moment later. "What are *you* doing here?"

She gasped. "What?" Her words came out as soft as an ephemeral spirit.

He shook his head. "How are you even *here*? You're supposed to be locked up like the monster you are."

Her heart sank. "But, we're married. We have a family."

He shook his head again. "I don't have a family. And I *certainly* don't have a wife." He slammed the door, the loud bang striking her like a slap.

Macey stood there for the longest time, not knowing what to say, what to do. What was there now? She'd never imagined in a thousand years, even with all her doubts and fears, that he would treat her like that. *I don't have a family.* The words reverberated in her skull, stinging each time they struck their mark.

She turned around and stumbled back to the SUV, her world in a tailspin.

What now?

Terra worried about Macey the entire way back to the caravan. Her friend didn't say a word, didn't make eye contact, and looked destroyed. She knew the conversation had not gone well. She didn't listen in, but she'd watched, and it didn't take eagle eyes to see the facial expressions that passed across her husband's face. He'd looked disgusted, like he hated her. That had to hurt.

They reached the parking area and Jackson turned off the engine, giving a heavy weight to the moment as the silence settled into their bones. Terra exited and ushered Macey from the car. Macey barely noticed the guidance as they made their way to Philippe's trailer, where he had a deer carcass stretched out over a table. With efficient movements, he cleaned the animal and dumped parts destined for the community hall in a cooler and offal in a bucket on his other side.

"It didn't go well." He stood as he spoke, his voice gentle and kind as they approached. He peered down at Macey with sympathy.

Terra shook her head, not sure if speaking it out loud would break her friend.

But Macey surprised her by lifting her chin high, drawing in a deep breath, and facing Philippe before saying, "I'm a widow."

Terra looked at her friend in surprise, taking in the shut-down, haunted look in her eyes, but kept her counsel. She supposed it was as good an option as any. Certainly, it should allow Macey and Beth to mourn what they'd lost and move on.

If they *could* move on.

———————

After they returned, everything seemed to fall into place. The new members of the community were adjusting, and Philippe had started making overtures toward Macey, who, while not completely open to them, wasn't closed off to them either. Philippe had been trying to connect with Beth as well and making more progress. Though she was still hesitant, Beth accepted him better than her mother did. Probably, she was so starved for a father figure that, even in her own quiet and reserved way, she welcomed what he offered.

All around Terra, people she knew and cared about were adapting, healing, but she just couldn't settle. Every day, she was eaten away by the things she'd heard. She'd lived in a bubble for far too long, first with her own willful ignorance, then at the shifter camp, then here at the caravan. She kept drifting into these mindsets where the outside world didn't matter, where it couldn't affect her. Then, every time her nose was pushed into the shit brewing in the world, she was shocked, motivated to act, and sick with the thought of how she'd lived until that point.

But it wasn't just her. Jackson did it too. His attitude bothered her. "It's none of our business," she griped under her breath. Was it, though? Sure, she understood and could even accept that sometimes you had to make change where you could, that sometimes a problem was just too big. Terra wasn't a leader, didn't know how to motivate people, and certainly didn't know how to initiate change.

So what could she do?

What *should* she do?

And would it make any difference?

She huffed as she stormed into the trailer, stomping into the office. On the wall, a dry erase calendar marked a day only a few days away when they planned to move to the next site.

Had it been that long already?

But it had been weeks since they'd rescued the others from the camp. They still had patrols watching for retaliation. She kept expecting something bad to happen, for people in uniforms to storm the caravan, rounding everyone up.

Terra collapsed into her chair, a padded folding job that wasn't comfortable, but didn't take up space when Jackson slept. She stared at the paperwork that needed her attention, at the computer for accessing the accounts and records. She wanted to be productive, useful, but her heart wasn't in it today.

To her left, a solitary window had its room-darkening curtains drawn open, letting in light. It also revealed a straight path to the community hall with the temporary tent peeking out behind it. Near the community hall, adults chatted while children ran in furred forms, more appropriate to the cooler weather. She flinched, hating her reaction yet again to facing the nature of this place.

She dragged her hand over her hair, pulling for good measure. Why couldn't she get her head around this? Why couldn't she accept this? "Gah!" She slammed her hands down on the desk, the flimsy material complaining ominously at the abuse.

Terra froze, hoping it wasn't broken, but it held and she let out a sigh of relief. She shook her head, resting her forehead on her palms.

"What am I doing?"

CHAPTER SIXTEEN

*J*ackson pulled the squeaky door to his trailer open, an action he took more and more pleasure in nowadays. It felt good having people to come home to, even if they weren't always there when he returned.

His head was filled with planning for the move now, his people packing and securing community resources behind him. Still, having Annie's things strewn over the couch or leftovers Terra'd cooked the night before waiting in the fridge put a lightness in his heart, drawing him from his thoughts.

So when he walked through the door and Terra stepped out of the office, he smiled. He couldn't help himself. It just made her scowl at him, though.

"Something wrong?"

What happened?

Where was Annie?

Was she okay?

Terra crossed her arms at him, shaking her head for good

measure. "We can't just hide in this little oasis you've created for us, Jackson."

He stilled, confused. "What do you mean?"

"It's none of our business?" She looked at him as if he should know what that meant.

Did she mean the shifter camp? Sure, he'd said that, but he'd also helped her free the others. She couldn't be mad at him for that, could she? He still wasn't sure it had been a good idea. He still had people monitoring the surrounding areas, expecting the government to find them, to come down and scoop them all up.

It was a mistake. You know it was.

Yet, he would have done it again, wouldn't he?

Terra didn't wait for an answer. "You say that about every-thing, everything outside of your self-imposed walls. Shifters in camps? Not our problem. Treaty with the Incirrina? Not our problem."

He stared at her, incredulous. "And what would you have me do?" he said, throwing up his hands. He felt powerless for the first time in ages. He didn't know what Terra wanted from him, didn't know if it was something he could even provide.

Her face fell, and he wished he'd kept his mouth shut. "I don't know. Something. We need to do something."

After that conversation, they didn't talk. It ate at Terra almost as much as when her bubble had popped, forcing her to act, to rescue the others from the shifter camp. She wanted to talk to Jackson, almost apologized a couple times, but she couldn't give the words voice. After all, she didn't mean them. She was sorry it had put distance between them. Even worse, Annie felt that distance, worried about them, tried to bridge the gap, which about killed Terra, but she wasn't sorry she'd said what she said.

It needed to be said, even if he didn't want to hear it.

She dropped onto Philippe's front stoop, wondering if the big guy would be around any time soon. Then again, Macey would be just as good. She couldn't decide if she needed Philippe's quiet wisdom or Macey's resigned realism right about now. Either would be welcome.

She got neither. A bear lumbered up to the front of the house, cocked its head at her, then ambled up to her and plopped its massive skull on her lap.

Terra looked at it wide-eyed for a moment before dropping her hand on its head and running her fingers through its long, brown fur. It rumbled in appreciation, and she smiled. "Maybe *this* was what I needed."

Jackson hated himself a little at the moment. Annie had started chasing him around, asking lots of questions, most of them having to do with why he wasn't talking to Terra. The girl was voracious, like a terrier, and completely adorable. Today, she was following as just that, a terrier, an improbably large terrier, but a terrier nonetheless.

He looked behind him. Yep, she was still following. Jackson kept adjusting his stride so she could keep up with him. If only Terra's needs were so simple. He didn't know how to please her. He didn't know how to fix this, but he'd broken them, and he needed to do the mending.

Around him, tents had been dismantled, outdoor furniture

were being stowed, and trailers closed up. At this rate, they could leave for the new site tomorrow morning, but his gaze did little more than run over the proceedings disinterestedly. In the past, he would have helped each person as he saw a need, directing them to higher efficiency.

Moving was always an exciting time, but he preferred to be settled, to watch as the life returned to the caravan, as their lives bloomed and stretched over the land, overtaking it in all their color and vibrance.

So watching it all packed away and broken down left him a little hollowed out this time.

Buh-rringg.

He jumped, the sound of an old telephone ripping him out of his funk, saving him from yet another downward spiral. "What?" he barked into the cell phone.

A voice he hadn't heard in some time came through the line. Many years ago, he'd offered a hand to a shifter who was strong, capable, but in the end, untrusting. She hadn't been ready for what he offered that day, so he'd given her his number, telling her he would be there, anytime.

He never expected to hear from her again, so her voice on the phone now was jarring, shattering his world without even trying.

"It's Mila. We have something to discuss. The fate of the world is in the balance."

PART TWO

"*Vanity and pride are different things, though the words are often used synonymously. A person may be proud without being vain. Pride relates more to our opinion of ourselves, vanity to what we would have others think of us.*"

— Jane Austen, *Pride and Prejudice*

CHAPTER SEVENTEEN

$\mathcal{T}$he door to the trailer opened, and Terra peeked out from behind the office door. Jackson stood in the doorway, holding it open. She was tempted to ignore him, return to her paperwork, but the look on his face stopped her. "What is it?" she said, standing up from her chair.

"I just got a call." He stared down at the phone in his hand, rubbing it absently with his thumb.

"What about?"

"Someone I met years ago. She's asking for my help."

She? Terra tamped down on the moment of jealousy. "What's she want?"

"She wants shifters to help save them from an alien invasion."

And she saw it, the purpose, that nagging feeling that made her fight with Jackson in the first place. She didn't know what this would mean, what would happen, but she knew they needed to act.

Then her mood turned dark, reality setting in. "And you don't want to do it." She glared and pointed a finger at him, furious over his obstinate insistence on non-involvement. How could he be so heartless, so cruel? How could he turn his back on billions of people as if they were nothing?

Not our problem.

His constant refrain popped into her head, working her into a lather, her frustration spilling out her mouth without thought. "You know, you might not trust humans, but those fuckers won't stop at the humans." She spread her arms wide. "These shifters you love so much, that you hold in such high regard, share this planet with them. We have to get along, we have to share. Sometimes that means putting aside our differences and past mistakes."

She scoffed. "But you don't want to get along. You just want to bury your head in the sand and hope it all goes away. I mean, they're still packing up out there, aren't they? You're *still* planning to pick up and leave, as if that'll solve *any* of our problems."

Her mind flitted to the camp, and she shivered. Was this a mistake? She couldn't go back, not to her old life, not to the camp.

"I could be sentencing everyone to the same fate as you." He looked torn, devastated, shaking his head. "I couldn't do that."

"Or you could be sentencing them to death." She shook her head in turn. "You're not a government, Jackson. You're just one man. You can let the others know what's going on, but you can't force them to help. This isn't on your shoulders."

"You want to hear them out."

"I do."

Terra wrung her hands, butterflies wrecking havoc on her stomach as she sat in the passenger seat, Jackson driving them to the meeting. It felt like Jackson had told her about the call only moments ago, but they'd been on the road for over an hour.

She let out a deep breath, telling herself that it would be fine. But they were meeting the military, and she struggled to make herself believe her own assurances. Her mind flashed back to getting screened for that secretarial job, to the puke green scrubs. She didn't know why that detail stuck in her head, but it did. That was the last time she'd been on a military base. That moment changed her life forever.

Then inevitably, her thoughts skipped to the day she'd been taken, men in suits dragging her out of her home, dumping her into a van and driving away. The hopeless certainty that it was a mistake. The helpless need to escape.

That hopelessness burned off into righteous anger, her heartbeat pounding in her ears. How dare they! For nothing more than the genes she carried, they locked her up and stole her life. No one had that right, but they used their fear to justify violating the very laws and rights they'd founded their country on.

But then, according to the laws, she wasn't human, so it didn't count.

Bullshit.

Her hands curled into fists at her sides, pressing hard into her thighs. Around her, shades of green whizzed by, intermittently interrupted by speckling shadows as light seeped through the branches of the trees they passed through.

"You could have stayed behind," Jackson said, taking his eyes off the road and looking pointedly at her fists. "I could handle this on my own."

But something inside her rebelled at that thought, unwilling to let him go alone, needing to have his back. "I'm fine," she said, but she was anything but fine.

———————

Jackson sat at a large conference table, Terra deceptively meek as a mouse at his side. He hated how she almost cringed at them like a prey among a pack of predators, and yet a seething, impotent rage bubbled under the surface. He wanted to take her away from this place, bring her back home where she could be safe with Annie.

His mood had soured during the long drive to Clark NSS Base as Terra's mood remained dark, fluctuating between fear and fury seemingly without pause or reason. To make matters worse, his skin crawled at being surrounded by so many humans, especially since they knew what he was.

He'd had his dealings with humans in the past, but always with the added armor of their ignorance of his true self. It kept him confident and allowed him to go about his business feeling assured that he and his people were safe from those he did business with.

Now, nothing was certain. He couldn't hide from the military, the government, any longer. Once he returned to his caravan, they would know, would follow his movements using all resources available to them. He'd lost his greatest armor —anonymity.

Bodies continued to stream into the room, settling into their places, chatting idly while sipping coffee. No one smiled. The air hung heavy with the seriousness of current events.

Then an older, sterner gentleman in a stark uniform marched in, walking to the head of the table. "Let's begin," he said as he took his seat. He steepled his fingers. "I'm told we have a shifter named Jackson here." He pivoted his head, zeroing in on one of the only civilians in attendance. "You understand the situation?"

"I doubt I've been fully briefed."

He nodded. "An alien military force is on approach to Earth, estimated to arrive in a matter of days. This force likely outmatches our military might in space and as such the battle will likely extend to ground forces. This is an event unlike any in human history, and as such, we are considering non-conventional approaches to the problem."

"You want to use shifters in the fight," Jackson said, his voice dark with anger.

Terra gasped at his gumption, and he clasped her hand, rubbing his thumb across the back.

"Yes, if they would be willing."

Jackson stalled, trying to sooth Terra with his touch. A part of him felt paralyzed, knowing that his next words would change the fate of shifters for all time. It was terrifying and thrilling at once. Terra's presence at his side encouraged him to jump in with both feet, but he hesitated. She would judge him if he refused. He knew that. She might even leave him, which left his chest cold and empty. But how would it affect his people?

He imagined his people, shifters, bleeding out and dead on the battlefields, fodder for the aliens' cannons. But he also imagined children running from their homes, screaming as they were gunned down. He had no illusions about the stakes. He glanced over at Terra, who curled into her seat, a fine tremor running through her, her anger having fled, consumed by fear.

There was no decision, was there?

"I can't guarantee any of the shifters will join the fight."

143

Terra looked over at him, her jaw slack.

"We don't have military or commands like you do. We are more like nomadic tribes than anything that organized. I can spread the word, coordinate, but I can't force anyone."

Jackson paused, not sure what he wanted to share. He didn't trust these people, had no faith in humanity or even their own self-interest. They would shoot themselves in the foot if they thought his kind were a threat. On that, he had no doubt. They'd done it countless times throughout history.

He leaned back, squeezing Terra's fingers without realizing. She patted his hand, smiling at him ever so slightly. That attempt to reassure him settled him. It reminded him of the responsibility he had, the custodianship he had over the people in his caravan, and over those he would soon be contacting to garner their aid.

He leaned forward, steepling his fingers like the big honcho had been doing from the start. Though the oldest and highest ranked human here, and as such the most respected, he was still a spring chicken next to Jackson. "I'm sure you know more than I can imagine about my people. You've probably experimented on those you held hostage over the years."

A few men squawked as if to object, but Jackson didn't let them.

"But I'll provide a few highlights, nonetheless. We are very difficult to kill when in reasonably good health. If we are to help, we will need significant quantities of calories and nutri-ents readily available. We will need all the resources that any soldier would receive, including weaponry and body armor."

A general across the table from him leaned heavily on his elbows. "But with your natural talents, wouldn't that be a waste of resources? The humans are a lot more vulnerable and will need those things more."

"Humans are not more vulnerable than shifters. Shifters can recover from injuries humans cannot, but they will sustain just as much damage, feel just as much pain. And before you say it, while we can do considerable damage with hand to hand combat, it still pales in comparison to an automatic rifle.

"What's more, most of us have no formalized training, which means we'll need some orientation before stepping onto the battlefield."

Some of the faces around him closed up into scowls. He suspected those opposed to this didn't like the direction this conversation was going. Tough.

Jackson stood, glanced to Mila, who'd made the call to bring him here, and nodded his head. She looked better than the last time he'd seen her ten years ago. They'd had the occasional conversation in that time, mostly in couched "theoretical" terms where she would ask about the experience of being a shifter, never willing to admit it openly.

She'd developed into a strong, confident woman. Though a slight uneasiness remained in her eyes, she didn't show it anywhere else. And the rampant paranoia from their first meeting was completely gone. "Keep in touch," he said before pulling Terra to her feet, turning his back to everyone, and walking out.

CHAPTER EIGHTEEN

"Wait up!" Mila said as they walked out of the building, her voice breathless from running after the two shifters. She jogged up beside them and smirked. "You know, that wasn't the end of the meeting, right?"

Jackson shrugged, as stoic as ever. She'd met him over ten years ago after she'd shifted for the first time. He'd reached out a helping hand, and she'd repeatedly swatted it away, too scared to see a good thing when it was right in front of her.

Not that it made a difference. He'd still helped her, saved her life, and she never forgot his number, always keeping it in the back of her head just in case.

I bet he never expected me to join the military.

And yet as she stood before him, she couldn't believe her eyes. He looked just the same, like a mountain that measured time in eons rather than years. Mila shook her head. "You haven't changed a bit, have you?"

"Not much," he said, his chin stuck out as if he were proud of that fact.

Mila turned to the woman at his side. "And you are?" she said, offering her hand to Jackson's compatriot, a striking redhead who acted shy as a mouse. She seemed calmer now that she'd escaped that insufferable meeting room. Mila couldn't blame her. After her first shift, being in a room full of military officers would have sent her into apoplectic shock.

"Terra." She grasped Mila's hand in a firm if slightly damp handshake. "Nice to meet you."

Mila just grinned. "Since you asked for an orientation, have your people call here for orders. The suits are still working out the details on coordinating ground troops between countries, but we can direct them to their nearest military base for gearing up and debriefing." She handed Jackson a card.

Jackson shook his head. "You never really needed us, did you?"

"Oh, I did, but good luck getting me to admit it." She smiled, no longer afraid. Ten years ago, she saw Jackson as a threat, someone to run from, to fight. "But thank you for offering. I may not have accepted, but thank you."

Terra had never realized how influential or connected Jackson was. He had seemed completely comfortable sitting in a room filled with humans he hated, barking orders at them. High-ranking officials at that.

They'd taken a roundabout way of returning to the caravan, spending three times as long getting home as getting to the base. She suspected he didn't want to be followed, but she didn't see how it was possible to avoid it. If the government wanted to follow them back to their people, they certainly had the resources to do so and without them the wiser.

147

Sitting in Jackson's small office, she marked off the next person on her list. They'd started as soon as they got home. Over the evening and next day, the list grew, tallying who Jackson had called, who'd agreed to help, and who was staying the fuck out of it.

She'd expected Jackson to be unable to withhold his constant hatred for humanity. She'd expected it would ooze into his voice, into his word choices, discouraging his equals from helping Earth, but the list of those agreeing to fight was growing.

Even so, Terra felt time slipping away. They only had days until the alien force would invade Earth, days to coordinate, to prepare. How could they ever succeed?

But she wouldn't tell Jackson that. She'd pushed him into this course of action and she needed to see it through, have faith in him, in their people. She refused to think of the consequences should they fail.

And yet the image popped into her head, anyway. Ships and flames filled the sky as missiles and bombs launched on both sides. The sky grew dark with death and the air filled with the sounds of terror and the smell of smoke and decay. She shivered, hating her active imagination, which had always thrilled in taunting her with worst-case scenarios.

Not now!

"Next?" she asked Jackson, putting all her effort into keeping her voice and face light. She smiled. He didn't need her negativity now.

Philippe sat on his front stoop, staring out over the packed-up caravan, holding Macey and Beth as they clung to him.

Around the caravan, the children were reserved, the adults resigned. None of them could have predicted Jackson's announcement last night when they returned, least of all Philippe. He'd known the man for years, had coached him on some of his worst tendencies many times over. He'd never expected the man to actually overcome some of them, especially not in so wholehearted a way.

At the announcement, many people shouted in anger, others in fear. Some had not even heard the news of the imminent alien invasion. One advantage of living in the middle of nowhere was they could choose to ignore the world around them. They could let the outer world pass them by and simply live.

Some were angry because Jackson had taken that away from them. Right here, right now, they couldn't simply let the world pass them by because he'd dragged it to their doorstep. He didn't demand that they fight, but he also didn't let them bury their heads in the sand either. They had to make a choice, and for once, Philippe was conflicted.

Ordinarily, he would have stepped up without a second thought, even without people knowing he was a shifter. He saw it as a duty, one he took pride in. Unlike Jackson, at least the Jackson he'd always known before, he saw clearly how the outside world could encroach on their oasis, dash their little utopia against the rocks. He had no illusions now about what would happen if the aliens landed on Earth.

But with the girls in his arms, he hesitated. Their small bodies shook with the terror and uncertainty of the near future. He needed to protect them, and he wasn't sure how to do that best. If he left, fought, he could keep them safe, but they would be alone, with no one here to comfort them. If he stayed, they would be comforted, but what if some of his people died because he didn't have their backs?

He felt trapped, and he pulled them closer to his sides.

What do I do?

Jackson stepped out of his trailer, taking a deep breath and stretching. It had been a long day, just over twenty-four hours having passed since the meeting with the military. "I don't care, Timmy!" Terra yelled. Somehow, Timmy had snuck in without him noticing. He hid a smile as Terra's grumblings filtered out through the thin walls. The little robot had been criticizing her organization techniques and providing feedback. The battle between woman and robot had raged pretty much from the day she arrived. He was curious to see how it would end.

Before long, the fight dissipated and the sounds of splashing and laughter drifted to him. Terra was giving Annie a bath. He looked down at his watch. He would have to start calling numbers overseas soon. They couldn't stop simply because it was getting late. Already, he felt sleep deprivation dragging at him. But the longer they took to call, the more people would be in danger, the harder it would be to organize the shifters.

Stepping off and down the lane, he wandered with his hands in his pockets. He was wound up, anxious. He didn't like it, but he didn't want to let Terra down. This was all for her, for Annie. But that wasn't to say he didn't see her point. She was right, of course, not that he would ever admit it. They shared the Earth with the wretched humans, and like it or not, they needed to defend it too if they wanted to survive.

"Ho there," Philippe called out, waving him over.

"Hello, old friend. You look troubled."

Philippe huffed, a self-deprecating smile pulling at his lips. "I find myself in a quandary."

"Oh? I thought *I* was the one always in need of *your* guidance."

Philippe laughed, the expression almost reaching his eyes. "I think we can leave off your neuroses for a spell."

"Then what's the problem?" Jackson sat down on a stump in the front yard, the uneven edge and splinters digging into his ass. He shifted in his seat, but it didn't help.

"I don't know what to do."

"What do you want to do?"

Philippe sighed. "That's the problem." He glanced back at his home, his shoulders slouching in defeat. "I can't do both."

"Tell me."

He looked Jackson dead in the eye. "I love Macey."

Jackson stared at his friend, not sure how to respond. "That was sudden."

"I imagine no more sudden than your love for Terra."

Jackson kept his mouth shut. He had no room to talk. He *did* love Terra, would do most anything for her. How stupid was that? "Then what's the problem?"

"She's fragile, jaded, hurt by her past. The pending invasion has only made her more so. I want to comfort her, protect her, but I want to fight as well, protecting her and *everyone* else."

Jackson nodded. Philippe had disappeared repeatedly over the years when he saw a just cause. He knew how the other man's mind worked. "Then ask her. Ask her what you should do, what she needs. She may tell you she needs you here, she may not be able to verbalize it, or she may tell you to go. You won't know until you ask."

Philippe shook his head, a great grin on his face. "When did you get so wise?"

"I reckon I learned it from you."

CHAPTER NINETEEN

*T*erra hated this. She'd started this mess, and now she would have to live with the consequences. She wanted to say stupid things like, "Do you really have to go?" and "Don't leave me." Instead, she stood tall, Annie hugging her leg as she tried to serve as a symbol of strength for the others left behind.

She stood in the center of the caravan, hard-packed earth unmarred by the brightly colored fabrics that had littered it before. It felt empty, like an uninhabited house. In every direction, she could see well beyond the trailers to distant fields and meadows. Trees still closed them in, but a far ways off.

She turned back to the gathering, running her fingers gently through Annie's hair. Both men and women hugged their friends and loved ones goodbye. Almost half the settlement, not including those rescued from the camp, had volunteered to fight. In a couple days, the battle would begin. How many of them would return home?

To her left, Macey clung to Philippe while he hugged Beth with both burly arms. He buried his face in the girl's neck, taking in a shuddering breath. She couldn't hear what they said, but it rang true in her heart. It was what she wanted to do as well.

But she didn't, because she needed to set an example. She didn't want to, but she had to.

That didn't stop Annie from racing into Jackson's arms and screaming, "Don't go!"

Terra gave him a lopsided smile as he picked up the little girl he'd adopted just as much as she had.

Looking Annie in the eyes, he said, "I'm coming back. Don't you worry. That's a promise."

Annie nodded, but buried her head in his shoulder. She sniffed and broke Terra's heart. She walked up, rubbing the girl's warm back through her clothes.

"It's okay, sweetie. He said he's coming back, and he will. What about all the other boys and girls who have mommies or daddies leaving? Don't you want to help them, be strong for them?"

Annie sniffed again, lifting her head from Jackson's shoulder, then looked around, seeing the whole scene for maybe the first time. She nodded, her face red and puffy from crying.

Terra smiled, proud of her. She rubbed her cheek with the back of her hand. "That's my big girl."

Annie smiled and rested her cheek on Jackson's chest.

"When do you have to leave?"

"We should probably already be gone, but this isn't easy for any of them. Many have never left the caravan, even for shopping."

She nodded. "But they'll have you. I have faith in you. You'll see them through this. I know it."

"And you'll see those left behind through this." He caressed her cheek, smiling at her, but it left her cold inside. "Be strong. They're going to need you."

"Jackson, I'm not a leader. I've only been here a short while. Why would they listen to me? Why would they *look* to me? I'm no one." She felt on the brink of hyperventilating, panic rising to choke her.

"You're mine."

She stilled. "Really?" she said, doubt edging her voice. She'd never been overly fond of the whole he-man, alpha crap in romance. You couldn't just declare a woman yours and be done with it, but she did like him, even if he drove her nuts sometimes.

"You're everything I want, everything I never knew I needed. And you're everything *they* need to get through this."

She shook her head, not wanting or willing to believe what he was saying. *I'm not a leader. I can't do this.* But he believed in her, had faith in her, and whether she liked it or not, he was leaving her responsible. She sighed. "Okay, but don't blame me if this place is a mess when you get back. Don't forget you're the one who left me in charge."

He smirked. "I'm sure I'll never hear the end of it."

"Of course not."

Jackson leaned in and pressed a feather-light kiss to her forehead. His dry lips were like angel's wings against her skin, begging her to hold her breath in the hopes that it would last a moment longer. "Until we meet again," he said, handing Annie off to her and walking away.

"You couldn't just say goodbye, could you?"

He turned around. "Goodbye is an ending. This isn't the end."

He walked toward the cars, disappearing out of sight as the lane curved between the trees.

Terra turned around, hefting Annie onto her hip. Around her, the people left behind milled about, not knowing what to do with themselves. She couldn't blame them. The caravan was packed for the move, and the entire place felt empty without the others. She had spent the last day or so doing nothing but helping Jackson reach out to his contacts all over the world, calling shifters to the cause. Now she felt listless, uncertain. He wanted her to help his people while he was gone, be a leader, but she didn't know how to do that.

I don't want *to do that.*

That's not me.

She rubbed Annie's back, the little girl holding the folds of her shirt in a death grip. Terra didn't know how to be a leader, but she sort of knew how to be a mother. "Well," she said, releasing a big breath, "that was a bit rough." She smiled, knowing nothing she said would reassure them, but maybe she could distract them, like distracting a child from an injury or illness.

But how? The thought plagued her, leaving her frozen in place as she continued soothing Annie in her arms.

"I'm hungry," Annie whined, attracting her attention.

"Are you?" Terra said with a smile.

"It's well past breakfast," Jemma said, moving up toward

Annie to bop her nose. The girl giggled, smiling a reward at Jemma.

"Come," an older woman said, clapping her hands. "We'll need to unpack the community hall."

Terra let out a sigh, relieved to have the burden of leadership taken from her shoulders for a while longer. As the caravan broke into action, she once more felt like an outsider, like she didn't belong. She put Annie down, letting her dash off to play while Terra hovered near the crowd of men and women who'd stayed, fruitlessly trying to find some way to help.

"Come on, children," a voice called off to the side, drawing the kids out of the way of the adults.

Terra stopped, watching as the woman started up a game that involved a lot of running and shrieking. As she stood there, everyone moved in concert, like a choreographed dance, working together without getting in each other's way. Everyone had a role. No one hesitated.

Everyone except me.

The call came at the wee hours of the morning. He rolled over in bed, grumbling to himself as the phone's shrill voice continued to assault him. "I'm up. I'm up."

He slapped his hand against the phone, triggering speakerphone more by habit than sight, and plopped back on the bed, rubbing his face with both hands to wake up. "Speak."

The person on the other end of the line hesitated before beginning. "This is *him*?"

He scoffed, wondering when he would stop having his time wasted by fools. "You're the one who made the call."

The voice hesitated again, and he contemplated going back to sleep. He looked over at the window, but no light leaked around the room darkening curtains.

"I have news of importance to the movement."

He sat up, resigning himself to having his sleep cut short. "Speak." He didn't like repeating himself.

"The military is planning to use shape-shifters."

He slammed his hand down on the wooden nightstand.

Those leftist sons-of-bitches.

CHAPTER TWENTY

Only hours after leaving the caravan, Jackson stood next to Philippe as they filed into the supply office at Clark NSS base, both of them still as boards. Soldiers called out directions, asking them to form lines, provide identifiers, accept uniforms, armor, weapons. Jackson waited at the head of the line, accepting each item without pause. He noted a patch on the shoulder of the uniform—a chimera with the words "Shifter Division" written underneath.

"Is this necessary?" he asked the man barking orders.

The man stood up straighter. "It's so the medics know what to do with the wounded. From my briefing, I was informed that shifters can heal fairly quickly with sufficient nutrients. Is that not correct?"

"It is."

He nodded. "The insignia is intended much like a diabetes bracelet—to inform medics what medical resources you need."

Jackson nodded, seeing the logic in the design, and moved on to collect the rest of his gear. Once finished, another soldier urged them down a side hallway and into a briefing room. Jackson and Philippe entered and sat at the front, waiting for the briefing to start.

Around them, their people trickled in, arms filled with gear, uncertain in this new environment. Many of them had lived largely rural or agrarian lives. This high tech, structured life-style didn't appeal to him, and made everyone else nervous and unsure of themselves.

Before long, the room roared with murmurs. A man of authority walked to the front of the room and cleared his throat, snapping his heels together to get the attention of the group. The crowd dwindled into silence as he dead-eyed them, demanding quiet, demanding respect.

"Better," he said, hands held behind his back as he started to pace. "You all know why you're here. In three days, an alien force will meet our space fleets above us. We are here to ensure that by then, you are prepared in the event they cannot repel the enemy."

The look in the man's eyes told Jackson all he needed to know. The officer didn't want to be here, thought this was a waste of time. He looked down his nose at the shifters who had agreed to come out of hiding, out of anonymity, in order to help protect their world. Jackson scowled, feeling an unfortunate similarity to the man. It left a bad taste in his mouth.

"I have to make you cretins ready for battle so you don't get good men, soldiers, killed." He glared at them, pivoting his head. In his gaze, he managed to broadcast that he thought he would fail. "You'll be split into squads. Each squad will be lead by a human military officer. You will follow his or her orders as if they are your own thoughts. You will not doubt. You will not question. You will not hesitate. Do I make myself clear?" He waited.

The room fell silent. Then it echoed with a dissonant, "Yes, sir."

"Good. At the back of the room is a group of officers. I will call each of your names. You will stand then file out after the officer by the door. That officer will own your ass until this clusterfuck is over. Do I make myself clear?"

"Sir, yes, sir," they said, this time almost as one organism.

"Good."

Terra sat down at the table in the newly set up community hall for breakfast, her "council" around her, helping her. Her hands flexed over a hot cup of coffee, the fumes and warmth soothing her. It was early and quiet, a sense of hesitance and anticipation in the air.

Yesterday had gone better than she'd hoped. They'd kept busy, though it was hard since they'd been planning to leave that day. Everything was packed. There were no crops to tend, no crafts to work on. A few of the adults wandered off to recheck the vehicles, make sure they were in good shape to travel. Others went off to hunt. The rest stayed behind with the kids. They'd managed to wear the children out last night, so they fell into a deep sleep as soon as their precious heads hit the pillows. A few had nightmares, came awake screaming for whichever parent or family member had walked away, but it could have been worse. It could have been much worse.

Terra zoned out as the men and mostly women discussed how to proceed until the others returned. All she heard was the murmur of voices, some deep and rumbly, others soft and gentle. Her gaze roamed as she took another sip of her coffee. They'd only done the bare minimum of setting up the community hall. They'd stacked the tables and chairs against the wall of the trailer, only setting out what they needed, and hadn't bothered with the tent that usually rose above it all. It gave them room to cook, sit, and eat.

As her gaze continued to roam, it stopped on Philippe's trailer, making her think of her friend. Macey was handling things better than she'd hoped. She and Beth were staying in Philippe's place, "looking after" the trailer as she'd put it yesterday. She doubted that was the real reason. But she didn't say anything. They were coping. That was all that mattered.

Terra was having a harder time. It had taken all she had not to cry herself to sleep last night, and the only thing that stopped her was Annie's little body sleeping so close. It would disturb the little girl, and she couldn't bear upsetting her. Jackson had asked her to be strong, but she didn't know if she had it in her. Every time she had an opportunity to be an example, to step up, to lead, she froze, doubting herself and her place here.

And what place is that? You can't even bring yourself to shift.

She was a fraud, an imposter, and these people deserved better. She couldn't even bring herself to open her mouth to speak, but she had to.

I have to do something.

But what could she do? "What else can we do to keep everyone busy?" she asked, trying to shake the melancholy. They needed to keep together, keep busy, and she needed to stop fretting over the chasm between herself and the caravan. They needed to forget about the others. The volunteers were safe for now. The enemy wouldn't arrive above for another couple days. There was no reason to freak out yet. They had time.

Jackson brought the rifle to his shoulder, taking aim. He took a deep breath in, feathering his finger over the trigger. With a breath out, he squeezed, a bullet punching into the middle of the target almost at the same moment the weapon bucked in his grip.

"Good," the sergeant in charge of their group said. "Again."

It was the first day of "training" and he stood elbow to elbow with other shifters at Clark's outdoor firing range. Behind the range, trees darkened the distance while blocky buildings rose tall on each side.

Pop. Pop. Pop.

Beside him, more guns fired, causing him to flinch each time even through the sound dampeners hugging his ears. He lifted the gun again to fire, a scowl forming on his lips.

Jackson and Philippe had ended up in separate groups. He didn't like it, wishing he could have his friend's back, but he kept his mouth shut, focusing on the task at hand. If they wanted to make it off the battlefield he knew was coming, they would have to focus, prepare. They didn't have long, only a few more days, and it was nowhere near long enough. Not at all.

———

Philippe dwarfed the small woman commanding their squad. But that didn't faze her. She barked out commands all day, running through drills until they managed to follow orders without thinking, without hesitating. He slowed, trying to keep pace with the much shorter stride of the officer leading them in a circuit around the base. Soon enough, though, he found himself almost stepping on her heels again.

She looked over her shoulder, unleashing her rage on him without a word. He would get an earful when they stopped.

Again.

It didn't matter. All that mattered was protecting Earth, protecting their loved ones. He thought of Macey and Beth, and he started to speed up again. This time, he stepped down hard on the officer's heel. She growled and stopped, yelling some unintelligible command to halt the procession.

"Drop and give me a hundred," she commanded, pointing at the ground as she glared at him.

Philippe dropped to hands and knees, his fingers curling into the prickly grass, and started the series of push-ups. It didn't bother him, didn't serve as punishment as it was intended. He felt bad that he'd stepped on her foot. But he'd never had to work as a team with someone so small before. In the past, he'd been grouped with men just as big as he was, fighting just as fast, just as strong. He'd never had to worry about stepping on *their* heels.

Terra stepped out of the trailer. It should have been just another day, but as she looked up, her stomach sank. It had been three days since the others left and she'd known it was coming, but she still wasn't ready. Her hand flexed on the edge of the door as red streams like meteors or shooting stars streaked across overhead. A patchy darkness blotted out the sky, hiding the sun from view except for the occasional rays peeking through.

It had begun.

CHAPTER TWENTY-ONE

*T*he radio crackled through the little shuttle, a constant background cacophony of battle, a reminder of what they fought for, who they fought with. Panic and determination bled through the airways, telling tales of which ships were doing well and which were losing.

Mila tuned it out, focusing on the fight in front of her. That was all that mattered now. She couldn't draw her attention away from the ships around her, keeping them one step ahead of the enemy. She dropped them into sub-space again, a dizzying swirl of colors as they jetted across to what should be the side of another enemy ship. *Hopefully.* "Ready," she called as Avery flexed his fists over the weapon controls. She sent them hurling out of sub-space with a flick of her wrist. The small shuttle shook with the barrage of ammunition being launched.

She smiled, smoothly shifting around the enemy. Then alerts triggered from behind her. "Shit," she said. "Craft approaching at six o' clock." Her hands flew over the controls, and she plunged them back into sub-space. They needed to get out from between two enemy forces. They would be road kill otherwise.

Coming out behind the new fleet, she hesitated, holding off Avery, as a message came over the radio in an automated translation, "This is the Incirrina battleship *Cirri*. We have received your distress call and are coming to your aid. We repeat, this is the Incirrina ship *Cirri*. We have received your distress call and are coming to your aid."

Luke tapped on the comms. "This is Communications Officer Hall of the Earth forces. Welcome to the fight."

As Mila glanced at her friend, she hoped they could understand him, but what did it matter? They weren't here to kill them.

We just might win this thing.

The Incirrina quickly drove the enemy toward the human ships, forcing them to take heavy fire. Cheers rang over comms as the tide of the battle changed before their very eyes. The darkness lit with weapons fire, pummeling the enemy from all sides. Adrenaline surged as the excitement of anticipated victory choked her.

A grin crossed her face.

We're got this.

Resistance proved more than they'd anticipated. The Morg officer frowned as his fellow ships failed around him, succumbing to the enemy. The damned Incirrina had arrived, determined to aid their hopeless allies. It wouldn't work. They had planned their vengeance for too long to be thwarted now.

But the battle in space was lost. An alarm blared, making him flinch as voices careened against each other in a discordant din that spoke less of confident authority than generalized panic. He scowled as he took in the view, ships battling against ships. He knew a lost cause when he saw it.

"Authorize the ground assault."

They hadn't seen *anything* yet.

———

Mila's mouth gaped as the enemy's ships seemed to explode before her eyes all at once. It defied sense, reason. Small chunks of the formerly massive vessels flew out, careening through space between the remaining battling spaceships. "Shit."

A moment later, the chaotic spray of metal shrapnel converged, streaming in a single direction—toward Earth.

Tristan leaned over her shoulder, "Fire at the pieces," he yelled.

Space lit up with weapons being discharged from dozens of ships hovering over Earth. Mila held her breath, gracefully avoiding the line of fire of any other ships while allowing Avery to fire at the impossible to hit specks.

A few exploded, but most accelerated, plummeting toward Earth, toward their friends and family, their homes.

God help us.

———

Something has changed, Jackson thought as he stared upward. Before, the ships amassing above had blotted out the sky with their bulk, the occasional flare of burning detritus streaking overhead. Now, the sky erupted in a display of fiery streaks to rival any Fourth of July celebration.

"They're coming."

Beside him, someone nodded right before a siren blared, calling everyone to their duty stations. Jackson took off at a run across the base, thinking of Terra momentarily before pushing her and everything else from his mind.

Today, they fought for Earth.

Jackson hovered in a transport vehicle, cradling his rifle, waiting impatiently to arrive at the coming battle. They hadn't left the base yet, the diesel engine still idly rumbling away to his left. Others in his shifter unit surrounded him as their officer sat in the front seat and out of sight, awaiting orders.

He looked out the back of the transport, but saw nothing but concrete and grass. He wished Philippe were there. The man had seen more battles than he could count, always following his conscience wherever it led. He would know what to say in this moment.

Without him, though, Jackson's nerves tensed, binding him up in anxiety and anticipation. His hand flexed harder over the barrel of his gun, feeling the cold metal compressing his flesh.

"Moving out," their leader's voice yelled over the engine.

The truck jerked to a start. *Where are we going?* He didn't know, and he wouldn't get any answers if he asked. Of course, in a way, he *did* know. They were going to the enemy, to where they'd landed. Soon they would spill out and take up the fight, spilling blood and taking lives. His heart sped up, and he turned to face the back, watching the base pass them by.

Before long, they slowed, and he recognized the area around the gate.

Then a rain of gunshots assaulted the air and competing voices drowned out the truck's engine.

"We're under attack," someone yelled.

"Fire. Return fire," the officer said.

Jackson stood and ran from the truck, turning in the direction of the gunfire.

Boom.

He flinched as heat lambasted him. Swiveling his gunsight, he found the security booth in flames, taken out by something big.

"Spread out! Spread out!" the order came, and the shifters reacted instantly, not needing to be told even once.

After all, standing out in the open was suicide.

He ran for the nearest cover, a copse of trees fifty feet from the fences. It felt like a lifetime, but moments later, he curled behind a tree, pressing into the rough bark as he sighted his gun around the trunk to locate the enemy.

Holes riddled the cloth cover of the truck, and the security booth continued to burn, but otherwise, nothing moved in the clearing between the trees flanking the gate.

We shouldn't have used this entrance.

After a few days on base, he knew it middlingly well. While he'd passed through at the booth currently on fire only days ago, another had no trees near it, preventing the possibility of an ambush.

Somebody fucked up.

Not that it mattered. He squinted, trying to spot hostiles in the quiet that settled over the *wrong* battlefield.

We don't have time for this.

He shifted his eyesight, needing to see better, needing to speed this up. For all he knew, aliens were landing as they stood here with their thumbs up their butts. He thought of Terra, of Annie, of his caravan. He couldn't let them down.

Scanning the opposite trees, he caught the telltale glint of sunlight on metal and opened fire.

CHAPTER TWENTY-TWO

"Mila, don't you dare," Tristan called.

Kyle glanced over as Tristan ran for his seat and flopped down, fumbling for the straps as Mila rocketed forward in the mad crazy style that reminded him of old school fighter pilots. She had a gift, careening around the ships with a single-minded intensity that he'd always respected and admired.

Still, as Earth loomed before them, his hands couldn't help flexing over the armrests as Luke whined in a seat to his left.

"You're going too fast," Tristan complained.

"No, I'm not. I think this is just right," Mila said as she continued to accelerate, pushing him back into his seat.

Kyle crossed himself, struggling to remember the prayers of his childhood as the ship rumbled, shaking them in their seats as it hit Earth's atmosphere. But she didn't try to slow down. He wanted to scream, but wasn't sure if it was in excitement or sheer terror.

Maybe both.

"Get ready, Avery," she said, rocketing forward at breathtaking speeds.

"You expect me to fire at these speeds?" But he gripped the controls anyway, his hands trembling.

"Absolutely."

He shook his head, but dragged in deep breaths, trying to focus.

Lines formed on the horizon, and he realized they'd looped the Earth. Small pieces of the enemy crafts streaked before them, lined up perfectly to be picked off by a decent shot.

"Fire," she said, never slowing as Kyle opened up a barrage at the alien menace before them.

Kyle grinned, wanting to laugh as his foe proved only too easy to hit this way.

God, this woman's brilliant.

The shuttle they drove wasn't intended for fighting in gravity, in atmosphere. It could be slow and difficult to maneuver. By accelerating, slingshotting around the Earth, she removed those deficiencies from the equation. They were like a missile locked on its target, destroying everything in its path.

He whooped as ships exploded before them, smoke turning visibility zero. Kyle tensed, waiting, ready.

"Mila," Tristan drawled a warning.

"No worries. I've got this." And she did. The main screen switched over to an alternative viewing option, showing obstacles in infrared. They passed straight through and out the other side.

The engines roared as Mila pushed the little shuttle further.

"Mila, no. That's enough."

Kyle tuned out Tristan's bleating, focusing on the task ahead.

"Bullshit. There's still more of them." Minutes ticked by as she pushed the ship harder, lining up a repeat approach on their enemy. "Ready."

"Ready," Kyle said, gripping the controls as his heart pounded an excited tempo in his chest. This time, it was anticipation that made his hands shake.

The streaks of enemy ships showed up again, and they all tensed.

The cockpit echoed as Kyle fired.

Fuck, yes! Take that!

Jackson stepped out of the transport vehicle that had seen better days, looking up. He didn't know what he expected, but little had changed. Fire still streaked the sky. The enemy still hadn't landed.

After the firefight they'd just left, he'd half expected to arrive to a bloody battle, but they probably weren't delayed more than ten minutes in total. He forgot how quickly battles tended to end.

As he hefted his rifle to his shoulder and jumped down, stepping up to the military officer leading them, he wondered who they'd been. Why did they strike? They'd been human. He knew that much. But why attack a military convoy on their own soil?

Or were they from another country? Were they an enemy of the United States? But then why would they choose *now* to strike, when working together meant more than ever?

They're human. That's why.

He'd long given up trying to understand the self-destructive tendencies of humans. They made no sense, were counterproductive, and he'd washed his hands of them long ago.

Still, now he was in the middle of their bullshit once more. Around him, the humans prepared for the inevitable, though he couldn't say he understood their logic. With hand gestures, he and his people were ordered behind the human troops as the sound of guns being checked and boots coming down hard on the ground filled the air.

He looked to the officer, a frown on his face, not liking the direction things were going. Meanwhile, his people looked to *him* for guidance. By his best guess, the military had estimated the ships would land a few miles outside the base, had coordinated troops to intervene, and evacuated civilians. As they'd driven up, he'd seen people racing in the opposite direction, running for their lives from a force they had no hope of escaping.

As he glanced around, encouraging his people with a look, he noticed that all his men and women waited behind the lines while the human soldiers stood before them, ready and waiting for the enemy to land. Their officers told the shifters to hold, to wait for their command. Jackson had the sneaking suspicion that a command to fight would never come, that they would rather their own people die needlessly than risk relying on shifters to save them, to defend them.

He scowled, not liking the nature of his thoughts or the reinforcement of those thoughts that stood in a line before him. While Jackson had never wanted to help humans, saw their flaws evident again and again in the actions they perpetuated against shifters and anyone they saw as "other," he'd shoved his prejudices aside for the greater good. It seemed not everyone had been so magnanimous. He didn't like it.

With a look, Jackson gave his people reassurance, encouraging them to follow the human leaders… for now.

The last of the enemy ships landed, their occupants flooding out, a sea of locusts on human soil. Human troops and war machines opened fire from below as Mila changed her game, and Avery did the same. Jets and bombers flew circles around her, taking out as many as they could. She shivered as soldiers fell, good men and women willing to die for their countries, for their families.

From above, she could differentiate the aliens from humans, but nothing else. The aliens crossed the grounds like a dark cloud, poisoning everything in its path, leaving death and destruction in its wake. The humans, on the other hand, blended into the environment, their camo uniforms designed for the terrain. Even the tanks blended somewhat with the landscape.

She circled again and again, feeling like a sitting duck, waiting for the enemy to start firing on her. The sluggish controls frustrated her, holding her back, and she wished she was still in space, where this bird could really fly. But the aliens had brought the fight here, to their home turf.

A proximity alert blared as a shot passed alarmingly close to her left wing. "Shit. Hold on."

Jackson waited, almost growling in frustration for the orders he feared would never come. Would they wait until all the human soldiers fell before calling on them? With each moment, his guilt ate at him, gnawing at his gut to do something. His people looked to him, their faces increasingly worried, anxious. Waiting didn't sit well with them either.

His ears rang from the constant barrage as he scanned the battlefield, reducing his hearing even as he enhanced his vision to see the distance and details better. It didn't look good. The firepower the aliens used plowed straight through their body armor. His allies took some down with them, but it took two or three times as many shots to down one of the enemy as it did one of their own. The tanks and jets could do significant damage, but it was a danger close mission, which limited their options. He glanced back at his people. "Fuck it."

Jackson took off at a run, increasing musculature and adrenaline as he lifted his gun to his shoulder, sighting along the barrel. He started firing before he even got close. *Pop. Pop. Pop.* Three enemies went down from perfectly fired rounds into the center of their foreheads right below the edges of their helmets. The thin edge of the trigger dug into his finger, keeping him grounded.

A round pummeled his shoulder. He grunted, gritted his teeth, but pushed on as he forced the wound to heal, to close. *Pop. Pop.* One more enemy dropped, another falling into his buddy, but staying on his feet. In his peripheral vision, his shifters followed his silent command, following him into battle. Sprayed dirt hit the side of his face as large artillery struck the battlefield once more. He flinched, but kept going.

His uniform stuck to his skin where he'd been shot, the blood hard to forget even when the wound had already healed. Flashes of light blinded him as an explosion erupted ahead, small but taking out a handful of the enemy. Jackson blinked, shooting blindly for a few moments until his vision cleared.

Like a a shifting tide, everything changed. His shifters dragged the fallen humans out of the line of fire, protecting them with their rifles and their bodies when necessary. A shifter dropped, not getting up right away. A retreating human grabbed him, pulling him up over his shoulders and dragging him to the medical tent.

Jackson turned his focus forward.

Pop.

Terra trailed behind as the last of them entered the caves. When the ground assault had seemed imminent, they'd picked up and left, heading here, where they hoped they could hide in safety. She thought of Jackson, who was currently or would soon be fighting them.

What was I thinking?

Why did I push him into this?

Anxiety gnawed away at her as she gripped Annie, comforted by her presence.

"Please be safe," Terra whispered under her breath. "Come home to us."

Ahead of her, one of the elders said, "Alright everyone. Settle down and let's set up our camps."

Terra stepped into the chilly entrance of the cave system, pulling her jacket closer around her shoulders as the briskness hit her all at once. In the dim light, people huddled together as children cried.

In the distance, the engines of distant jets and spacecraft roared, upsetting the sanctuary they prayed this out of the way place would be. Terra held Annie's hand tighter, tempted to lift her into her arms, as the little girl stared up at her in question. She looked down. "Everything'll be just fine, sweetie. I promise."

She just hoped she could *keep* that promise.

Jackson's mind kept flitting back to Terra. Was she safe? Was she scared?

Stop it.

He refused to dwell on that. He had people here who needed him. Especially since the human officers were useless to them. They'd yelled at their backs when the shifters dashed forward.

Did other shifters around the world face the same?

It didn't matter.

He alternated between fighting on the front lines and falling back to direct his people. As time passed, a rhythm developed. Men and women fought for a spell, using all the skills at their disposal to take out the aliens while trying as best they could to avoid fire.

But the enemy were thick before them, their black armor like an ever-shifting sea, and operating at this level was exhausting. Each of them grew tired, took shots they couldn't avoid, got sloppy. When that happened, he called them back, directing them to the medical tent where they could refuel and patch themselves up if need be. Some had to be carried off the field, but fortunately not many.

If they could keep this up, they might have a chance.

Maybe the world *would* have a chance.

CHAPTER TWENTY-THREE

The silence took Terra by surprise. For hours, the air was filled with explosions, roaring engines and cracks of gunfire. The caravan huddled together, distracting themselves as best they could, but they feared making noise as much as they feared for their loved ones. If they were too loud, would the enemy find them, capture them, kill them?

It ran through most everyone's heads, and the hours of constant sonic barrage mixed with the drifting scent of violence kept them on edge. So when it ended, they all stopped breathing, their bodies tense, waiting for it to start up again.

It didn't.

For a while, her ears rang with the remembered cacophony, but before long she caught the dripping of water. Deep shadows flickered around campfires which barely chased away the bitter cold and illuminated only enough to reveal the dreary grays of the cave walls.

Annie peeked out from under her arm, looking up at her with hopeful, trusting eyes. "Is it over?"

She smiled down at Annie, but the expression pulled at her, difficult in the wake of the uncertainty. The battle had ended, but who won? Was Jackson safe? Were the others?

Uncertainty surrounded her, every face asking, "What now?"

In a quiet voice, she said, "We'll stay here. Until we have news of what happened, we'll stay here." Shifting in her seat, she looked around. "Who's got the radio?"

Terra had made sure they brought a radio, figuring in the aftermath, it would be their only source of information. It wouldn't work in the cave, unable to get a signal, but she'd also brought headphones, and if they were careful, they could reach the mouth of the cave without risking exposure.

"I have it," one woman whispered, raising her hand as if they were in school.

Terra nodded, standing up and carefully crossing the uneven floor of the cavern. "Thank you," she said as she accepted the radio from the other woman's hands. "I'll see if there's any news."

Many people nodded, and she took a deep breath. "Annie, stay put."

Annie's lip pouted out, shuddering in that way little kids had of manipulating adults. "But…"

"No buts," she said, kneeling down on Annie's level. "I don't know if it's safe out there, kiddo, okay?" She touched the girl's cheek. "I need you safe."

The girl sniffed, but the woman she'd taken the radio from rested her hand on Annie's shoulder. "I'll keep her safe."

Terra nodded, smiling in thanks, and walked gingerly across the rocky terrain, careful not to trip as she exited the dim environs of the cave system. As she stepped closer to the outside world, a stiff wind brought with it smoke and warmth.

At the edge of the cave, she knelt down behind a bush, unnerved by the flames tinting the sky orange in the background. She plugged the headphones into the radio and clicked it on, scanning channels for news. For anything.

White noise filled her ears, interspersed with music from stations too far away to hear clearly. She kept scanning, but didn't hear anything resembling news. Switching to AM, she started again. Voices this time, a talk show declaring the end of the world. She moved on. More music. *Keep going.* Then she recognized something useful. NPR. She fiddled with the dial until it came in semi-clearly.

"We're still getting reports from correspondents around the world." Static crackled, blocking out words, obscuring them into nothingness. "The alien forces have been defeated in some places while battles roll on in others. Please, stay in your homes or shelters."

That was all she needed to hear.

It wasn't over.

———

Jackson stood surrounded by his people in the quiet that signaled the end of the battle. It lasted for a few heartbeats before his ears adjusted, returning to normal. Then the real aftermath of war greeted him. Blood, death, and weapons' discharge tickled his nostrils while the cries and moans of injured soldiers drifted on the breeze. Smoke dispersed, revealing more clearly the ground covered in black,

Bodies.

His stomach twisted, hating the necessity. He'd lived a

peaceful life, even if he'd lived with hate in his heart for far too long. At least he could say that hate had never turned to violence. He had no idea why they'd attacked, why they'd singled out Earth to conquer. It didn't matter. It was simply tragic. A waste.

Around him, his people waited for orders. "Search for wounded and bring them back to the medical tent. Once that's done, secure the enemy survivors." He didn't know what the human militaries would want them to do if there were any survivors, but international laws dictated they be taken as prisoners of war.

His mind strayed to Terra once more as he dropped his rifle to his side, and finally he didn't have to push the thoughts away. No enemy waited on the horizon, no one was in danger. He didn't know if more enemy forces would show up, but for now, there was a moment of peace. He wanted to go home, hold her, pick up Annie, see his people safe and sound.

Jackson turned and walked to the command tent. Stepping up, he saluted. "Is there any news?"

The man with the most bars on his uniform looked up at him and glared. "If you were military, I'd court marshal you for that stunt you pulled today." He stared hard at Jackson, but an understanding crossed the other man's eyes, gratitude. He would never admit it, but he was grateful for Jackson breaking rank, saving his men. "We're hoping to hear soon."

"Jackson!" Mila said in surprise as her gaze landed on a familiar face in the background. She stormed down the landed shuttle's ramp.

Jackson pivoted, orienting himself to her calling his name.

Mila picked up speed. She jogged across the expanse, glad to see him in one piece, even if they'd never really been friends. "It's good to see you," she said as she approached, reaching out a hand.

He gripped her forearm, nodding. "And you. What are the chances, huh?"

"How did you fare?" Mila wasn't sure she wanted to hear if shifters had died. They weren't her friends, she didn't know them, and she'd never connected with any shifters, always keeping herself aloof, but still...

"I don't believe we lost anyone. The military was better prepared than I would have hoped."

A dark look crossed his face, and Mila wondered what it meant, what he didn't say.

Again, she wasn't sure she wanted to know.

Terra stepped from the cave again, radio in hand. The smoke had cleared, and the world around her had returned to the natural serenity she expected. Blue sky rose over the trees that, more and more, were emblazoned with fiery colors. She plugged the headphones into her ears and turned the device on. A commercial played, trying to con people into buying the latest extravagance, which she found especially satirical in the current situation.

After a few minutes, the commercial ended, and the announcer spoke up. "There are continued reports of isolated pockets of fighting, but some areas have been cleared of the alien threat. These areas include. the US and Canada, Europe, and China. We have received no reports from Central or South America and sporadic reports from Africa and the

Middle East. Asia has mostly eradicated the threat, but there is still fighting in most countries on the continent.

"Around the world, reports have been consistent, though the information remains unclear. In all accounts, a few squadrons of soldiers, often times the second string, proved the key to the victory.

"These brave men and women were often seen fired upon, injured, and in many instances, they continued to fight long after their compatriots fell. Many war correspondents claimed that these individuals seemed to move at speeds they'd never seen before, returning to the battle even after grievous injuries.

"Some have theorized that these brave heroes were, in fact, shape-shifters or possibly the result of military experimentation. We'll keep you apprised as more details come through."

Terra clicked the radio off, wrapping the headphones around it. *Shifters.* She had no doubt. She didn't think hard on what this could mean for them. What did it matter? What mattered now was they could leave these frigid caves.

Tucking the radio under her arm, she ambled into the cave toward her people, not bothering to be quiet this time. There was no need. It was over. "Come on, everyone," she said as she approached. "The coast is clear."

There was hesitation, the moment stretching as they absorbed the news, then everyone stood, the children jumping to their feet and shrieking in delight. Terra smiled, stepping up to help people collect their belongings.

When would Jackson return home?

CHAPTER TWENTY-FOUR

*M*ila wrung her hands, wanting to bolt as she stood in front of the office door for the Commandant Commander United States Space Command, Admiral Brad Lewis.

Remember: No more running. You promised.

She'd received the summons as she was returning the battle shuttle.

Report immediately to Admiral Lewis's office.

The words still chilled her. She stared at the bold letters on his door, trying to con herself into bravery. Many people thought she was brave, but it was easy to be brave in the heat of the moment, when the enemy was breathing down your neck.

She shivered, feeling her courage evaporate. Everyday bravery was an entirely different beast, though. In those things, she'd always been a coward. So reaching up her fist took monumental effort, and she hovered there, her knuckles inches from the door's solid mass. Fear and anxiety raced through her, a nameless villain defeating her from the inside out. A villain who had defeated her more times than she could count.

"Fuck it," she said, smacking her knuckles against the surface a couple times, her heart pounding in her throat.

"Come in," a familiar male voice said from the other side.

Mila took a deep breath, embracing the "fuck it" she'd just said out loud. "Sir?" she said as she entered, standing tall with her hands behind her back.

"Sit."

Sitting made her even more nervous, at a disadvantage. It would be harder to flee, to fight. Not that she was thinking of doing either.

Don't kid yourself.

"What's your real name?"

Mila froze, ice rushing through her veins as the careful house of cards she'd built tumbled around her. She'd been caught. It was over. She would never fly again.

I should have known this was coming. Of course, he knows. He asked me to call Jackson, didn't he?

Oddly, despair filled her instead of the expected fear. She thought of Tristan, the future she'd never truly believed they could have. They wouldn't now, no matter how much he wanted it.

Would they lock her up? Send her to one of the camps? She couldn't remember, but impersonating a member of the military was a few years in prison, wasn't it? Maybe Tristan, her friends, would visit her. The thought made her heart lift a little.

For the first time, she realized just how tired she was. Mila had been running for so long. She didn't want to run anymore. She didn't have the energy. "Mila Dragomirov," she said, sealing her fate. She wouldn't run. Not again.

I promised, didn't I?

But he only nodded at that news and started typing away at his computer. "Mila Dragomirov. NSS Pilot Program. Passed sub-space qualifications with record scores." He sounded impressed and turned to her. "I'm assuming you took over for the USS *Orleans* mission." He paused, looking her dead in the eyes. His stare asked a question his lips didn't speak.

"Yes, sir. She died in a mugging shortly before the mission began."

He didn't seem surprised, which she found odd. Almost no one knew about the mugging. "You'll be properly rewarded for your actions, Pilot Dragomirov, and I'll start the paperwork to have your records transferred from the Pilot Program to NSS active service."

Mila's mouth fell open, not capable of believing her ears. Rewarded? She wouldn't be punished? She wouldn't have to hide, to lie? "Come again?" Her voice squeaked on the last syllable.

He stared her down, his face an expressionless mask. "You're dismissed."

She nodded, floating up from her seat and out the door. Her mind operated on autopilot, not seeing her surroundings or registering where she went. She arrived at her front door without remembering any of the steps in between. She could have been hit by a car and wouldn't have seen it coming.

Slipping inside, her footsteps pounded on the flooring.

"Are you okay?" Tristan said, suddenly there, holding shoulders, searching her eyes for answers.

She looked up at him and smiled. It felt like a shroud had been lifted from her, one that had covered her for over ten years. "Yeah, I think I am," she said with wonder.

187

Mila stood in the hallway, uncomfortable in her new uniform. She rubbed at the nametag where "Dragomirov" was spelled out in neat lettering like a blazing billboard crying out, "Shifter! Fraud!" She resisted the urge to cover it with her hand.

It had not even been a day since the battle to defend Earth ended. Hell, there were probably still pockets of fighting around the globe. It felt strange to be standing in a dress uniform in a crisp, clean government building while what sounded like hundreds of voices murmured in the background.

"Mila," Jackson said.

She turned, surprised to see him once again. They'd spoken over nothing but phone calls for ten years and now seemed to bump into each other at every turn. "Jackson. Good to see you again."

He walked up to her. "Do you know what this is about?"

She shook her head.

He glanced down, his eyes widening. "That's not the name that was on your uniform the last time we met."

She looked down, rubbing the spot again, a smirk on her face. "No, it's not."

"They know?" He looked sad.

"It's a good thing. I think."

He arched a brow at her, not saying a word.

She turned her back on him. Having enough cynicism for the both of them, she didn't need his to amplify it. From her position, she could see the podium where microphones sprung out like branches on a tree. The media swarmed in the audience, eagerly talking amongst themselves, chatting with friends or sharing suspicions about the press conference's topic.

Mila didn't have a clue. Though, looking at Jackson, she figured shifters had to play some role. Otherwise, why ask two shifters to attend?

From her right, a parade of people stormed down the hall, and a couple Secret Service agents ushered her out of the doorway, giving them room to pass. She just barely recognized the President from passing TV broadcasts on the streets.

What the fuck? She'd been called to a press conference being held by the President?

Her eyes rounded and mouth gaped just a bit.

"You're catching flies," Jackson said, leaning into her ear.

That brought her back in a blink. She snapped her jaw shut and turned, glaring at him. That he was right just made it worse.

"My fellow Americans," the President said into the microphones, silencing the crowd. Behind him, a line of men sat, mostly in military dress uniforms. "Our country, our species, our *world* has just survived a monumental occasion. In the last few days, we fought off a military force not of this Earth, fighting alongside allies of different countries, different species, even of a different planet. We worked in harmony, without prejudice."

Jackson snorted. Mila jabbed him in the stomach with her elbow, glaring at him again for good measure.

"By this cooperation, we won the day, saved our world, protected our families, our liberties, our lives. Without the assistance of those different from us, those we haven't always seen as equal or seen eye to eye with, we would have failed, would have lost.

"This day, I give thanks to the Incirrina, who unfortunately cannot be here in person, the countries of the world that looked past their differences in favor of a common goal, and the shape-shifter community, who stepped forward in spite of the risks to their own freedoms and liberties. The courage those young men and women showed in volunteering for combat, fighting for countries that had stolen their freedoms and imprisoned or even killed them, cannot be understated.

"As such, I thus avow that I intend to enact laws to give shape-shifters the same rights as any American citizen and resolve the issues that their abilities make in society. What's more, starting today, all shape-shifters currently in camps will be released, with reparations and redress to follow."

He turned to the doorway where Mila and Jackson stood, urging them to come forward.

The President smiled. *Fuck, what's his name?* "Shandor Jackson, when called, you rallied the shape-shifting community together, serving as a liaison, leader, and soldier in the war against the alien menace. For that, the world will forever be in your debt." He shook Jackson's hand, earnestness in his gaze.

Shandor? His first name is Shandor?

Then he zeroed in on Mila. *Oh shit.* Her palms started to sweat, and she resisted the urge to rub them against her pants. "Pilot Mila Dragomirov has repeatedly shown selfless courage in the face of unthinkable odds, putting her life and liberty on the line for others. On board the USS *Orleans*, she flew beyond all expectations to protect her crew and fought against an invading force to repel them when they threatened not only the crew but also the mission, a mission which contributed to the alliance that helped save our planet. She was also instrumental in the mission which finalized our alliance with the Incirrina and brought the early detection required to organize forces against the threat to come.

"During the battle to save Earth, she also piloted a battle shuttle into the fight above, taking out countless enemy craft, and continued the fight in atmosphere even though her craft wasn't designed for that type of combat. For that reason, the United States, the world, owes her a debt, and she will be awarded the Medal of Honor in formal ceremony next week for her gallantry."

The President lifted his arm in salute. Her mind blanked, shocked, but she lifted her arm in return, her chest tight with emotion.

Holy shit.

It's not over yet.

Those words rang through his head as Kyle stared Wilhem down where he sat on the cot in the prison cell.

It's not over yet.

Kyle waited, waiting for an explanation, waiting for answers. From the information he'd gathered, an incident years ago had destroyed Wilhem's voice, leaving it the scratchy, barely audible mess it currently was.

It also meant the criminal wasn't accustomed to speaking. His contacts had told him his brother, Niklas Wolf, had been the talker, the one people negotiated and conversed with. Wilhem was the brains, the skill, to Niklas's brawn and mouth.

So he didn't expect the fucker to open up easily or use a ton of words.

The battle was over, they'd won, in spite of the Wolf brothers' interference, but it would never truly be over for Kyle until he got his "man." He couldn't rest knowing there were traitors out there, people willing to kill, to sacrifice even the human race, to see their mysterious ideals met.

Kyle even wondered if the attacks on the shifter units might have been the same group. He'd heard about those events second hand, but security men did love to talk, especially to a compatriot stuck in the hospital. It was amazing how he could show up at Kaufman's bedside and get the scoop on half the active investigations in the NSS.

So he knew that while those attacks had been poorly organized and manned, they'd been well funded. The weapons recovered had been top notch, expensive. They'd had access to a few weapons not available to the general public, which made him practically drool at the investigative opportunities there, but it wasn't his case.

He refocused on Wilhem. Moments had ticked by in silence since Wilhem's latest statement, but Kyle didn't move, didn't rush him. He just glared.

Wilhem laughed, the sound cracking in his damaged throat, and shrugged. "I can't help myself. It's what I do."

What's he talking about?

Kyle resisted the urge to frown, leaning into his patience, his determination to get this bastard to crack.

"After receiving the job, I hacked the clients. I like to know who we're getting into bed with, know if we're likely to get stabbed in the back." He looked up at Kyle and shook his head. "They've got a hard on for your pilot like you wouldn't believe. They hate her for foiling their plans, blame her."

And she did it again, didn't she? She helped stop the sabotage on the moon and then got praised for it in a press conference just that morning. They attacked her shortly before the *Dakota* mission, didn't they?

And what the hell's gonna stop them from doing it again?

PART THREE

"Hell is empty and all the devils are here."

–William Shakespeare

CHAPTER TWENTY-FIVE

*M*ila sat, staring at her food for once instead of eating it. The announcement from the press conference continued to rattle around in her head. Though she couldn't remember the exact words, the President's face, or who attended, the words "Medal of Honor" kept rolling through her mind on a marquee.

"Well, this is a sight," Tristan said as he strolled in behind her, sidling up to the table. "Are you sick?"

She looked up, seeing the concern etching his face, and laughed. "No, I'm not sick. Just distracted."

He sat down across from her, his fingers tapping against the wooden tabletop, drumming away in a steady beat. "Must be *some* thoughts."

"Yeah." Her focus shifted internally again.

Medal of Honor.

God, how the hell did this happen? She didn't deserve a medal. She deserved to get thrown in prison for impersonating a member of the military.

Heavy hands wrapped around hers and she jerked her head up. "You *are* worthy, Mila."

She smirked. "It's gonna take me a while to believe that."

He patted her hands and leaned back again. "Of course, but don't forget. We all believe in you. We have from the start."

Mila stuffed something soft and chewy in her mouth to keep from talking. She knew the next word to pass her lips would likely start an argument.

Bang.

They both jumped in their seats, looking up at each other in question. "What the hell was that?" she said, turning to face the noise.

The back door.

"I don't know." He stood, turning toward the sound as well.

Then, men in black swarmed the room, brandishing weapons.

"Shit!" Mila yelled, jumping to her feet as she flipped the table and knocked Tristan to the side as a gun zeroed in on him.

Then the gun arm pivoted, targeting her. "No fucking shifter's getting the Medal of Honor," the man growled, a sneer on his lips.

Fuck.

Kyle stopped with a squeal of breaks in front of Tristan and Mila's place. As he turned in his seat, an uneasy feeling settled in.

It's too quiet.

Was he too late? Too early? Maybe Wilhem had been wrong?

Then he castigated himself. Wilhem didn't *know* they would attack. He didn't know their plans, though he imagined if he'd asked, he could have gotten the bastard to hack their systems and get specific information.

He cursed under his breath. That's what he should have done. He should have convinced him to help gather intel under the supervision of a cybersecurity expert, monitoring his web traffic. Instead, he'd gone off half-cocked, dashing off to check on his friends at even the *hint* of danger.

So fucking stupid.

When had he lost his edge?

Crack.

Kyle jumped, jerking his head toward the house as the single gunshot reverberated through the neighborhood. He popped his seatbelt and jumped from the car, not even bothering to close the door as he barreled forward, trampling the grass in the front yard as he ran for the door.

He burst through, stalling just inside the entrance. In the front hallway, everything looked normal. All was quiet again. Should he call out? What if there were still hostiles inside? He pulled out his pistol and lifted it into the air, then systematically searched the house.

To the right, the living room was clear, empty and undisturbed. He stopped in a doorway to the left. Mila stood in the center of the dining room with a gun shaking in her hand. She was covered in blood with drops plopping onto the ground from the fingertips of her left hand.

Around her, food was strewn everywhere, the table flipped on its side and riddled with holes. Blood soaked the floor, and he counted at least two bodies not moving.

"Is he? Is he?" Mila stammered, trying to finish a sentence but seemingly unable to complete the thought.

"Mila? What happened?"

Where's Tristan?

And then her stuttering sentences made sense. Kyle spotted a set of legs peeking out from behind the table and holstered his gun, dashing forward. He squatted at Tristan's head. Tristan looked pale and wasn't moving. For a second, Kyle wasn't even sure if he breathed.

"Is he?" Mila said once more.

"I don't know."

Then Mila collapsed, her body thumping against the floor. Kyle jerked to his feet, torn.

What the hell do I do now?

Kyle paced the waiting room of the hospital.

Mila will be all right.

That thought was easy to believe. Mila was a shifter. A little food, and she'll be right as rain.

Assuming they can get her to eat.

After the initial panic had worn off, he'd called 911. Tristan was bleeding, but breathing. He did the best he could to staunch the bleeding before checking on Mila. She was in better shape. Injured, but he didn't fear for her life. He quickly returned to Tristan's side, putting more pressure on his wounds and reassuring himself that Tristan still breathed.

So he wasn't too concerned about Mila, but Tristan was

another story. They'd immediately sent him through to surgery.

A doctor in a white coat stepped into the room. "Kyle Avery?" he asked.

Kyle jerked to attention, approaching with a click of heels as if he were responding to a superior officer. "Yes?"

"Ms. Dragomirov is awake. She should be released later today. You can go see her now. She's in room 103."

"Thank you, doctor."

He nodded and disappeared through the swinging double doors.

Kyle approached the nurse's station adjacent to the waiting room. "Where's room 103?"

The man at the counter pointed down the hallway to his right. Kyle followed the directions, startling when he entered the room only to be faced with someone he didn't know.

The patient smirked. "New girl's in the bed next to me."

"Thanks."

"Avery?"

Kyle walked past the curtain separating the two beds and stood at the foot of Mila's hospital bed. "The one and only."

She tried to smile, but the expression trembled, too much effort for her to manage.

It surprised him, so contrary to everything he'd known about her from the moment they met. She was strong-willed, stubborn, and courageous. She did what needed doing and sometimes bent the rules to do so. Seeing her so badly shaken disturbed him. He sat down on the end of the bed. "Hey, you okay?"

Her shaking hand went up to brush her loose hair back. "Yeah. I will be. Any news on Tristan?"

He shook his head. "Not yet. I'm sure he'll be fine."

She nodded her head, then stared out the large picture window. "They did it because of the Medal of Honor."

"What?"

She still didn't look at him, dropping her shaking hand to brush over the ugly hospital johnny. "They said no shifter would get the Medal of Honor."

Kyle leaned forward. "Can you tell me what happened?"

"They broke in through the back door. I pushed Tristan out of the way, then the guy pointed a gun at me, fired. He winged me and I attacked, managed to knock the gun from his hand. We struggled. There were gunshots, but I don't remember more than the sound of it. I knocked that one out and charged the other, struggled for the gun, then it went off." She turned to him. "Did I kill both of them?" She looked distant, almost haunted.

"I don't know. I didn't check. Didn't care."

She nodded and turned to face the window again, not saying another word.

Kyle stared at her, wondering if the same organization was responsible for this attack as for the *Orleans* and *Dakota* mission sabotages. But then, prejudice against shifters was practically a national pastime. It could be anyone who decided she didn't deserve the honor.

Except, his mind nagged him with a teasing thought; she wasn't the only shifter acknowledged at that press conference. Shandor Jackson might not be receiving a Medal of Honor, but the President had certainly made a spectacle of him.

Jesus Christ.

He stood up, but Mila didn't even notice. "I have to go." He left the room, pulling out his cell phone to make some calls.

Maybe Mila wasn't the only target.

Terra felt lost as they returned to the caravan site. Around her, the trailers and such stood sentinel, like abandoned buildings long after the residents had died or moved away. It was eerie. So was the hesitant way everyone entered, almost afraid to return to normal life, almost like they *couldn't.*

Then again, the others, the volunteers, still hadn't returned.

Will they return? Will the military, the government, let them?

She rubbed her face, not liking the direction of her thoughts.

My fault.

If they never returned, it would be all her fault. *She'd* convinced Jackson to volunteer, to organize the shifters. *She'd* told him they needed to step up, to do their part to save the planet. Had she been wrong?

She didn't want to believe that. She wanted to believe Jackson would come around that bend any moment now with the rest and her own failings would be forgotten, lost to the passage of time.

Annie was bouncing about, smiling and trying to get the other kids to join in her play. Some looked to their parents in askance, uncertain in the face of all this change. Others were still being gripped by their parents like a lifeline. But that didn't stop Annie. She dashed forward, glad to finally be free of that miserable cavern.

Terra couldn't blame her. It had been cold, wet, and dreary, perfectly matching everyone's mood as they waited to hear their fates. Now, she watched the blue, cloudless sky, but her mood still felt gray. The sky felt wrong, like it was acting out of character.

Then a sound. Footsteps came from the area where the caravan parked their cars, and her heart jumped in her chest. She glanced over, her feet taking her a few steps closer even before she registered the impulse.

Annie, having heard the same sound, squealed and raced forward, eager to greet everyone returning. Terra smiled, finally feeling like all was right with the world.

Then a shadowed figure stepped from the trees.

I don't know him.

"Annie!" she screamed, but it was too late.

More men in black surged from the woods, raising their weapons, and Annie was right in front of them.

CHAPTER TWENTY-SIX

*T*erra curled her arms around Annie as fear consumed her. All around her, the caravan sat on the cold, hard earth while men in black patrolled.

What are they waiting for?

She didn't get it. That scene continued to play out on repeat in her head. Annie running across the ground, kicking up leaves as she raced to who they all thought was Jackson and the others returning from battle. Then the men appearing, deadly efficient and well-armed. Annie sliding to a stop at one of their feet as Terra screamed, but they'd barely paid her any mind.

Instead, they'd stormed forward, corralling the adults, yelling slurs and curse words when they didn't move fast enough. Panic and pandemonium reigned as they were pressed together, body slamming against body as they fruitlessly try to escape their captors. Only they'd caged themselves instead.

Why did they attack?

That thought kept plaguing her. It didn't make sense, and her mind kept coming back to it, probably to escape everything else. If she kept wondering *why*, she didn't have to see the looks the others were giving her. If she kept wondering *why*, she wouldn't have to think about what would happen to her, to Annie, to them all.

But she couldn't escape the pleading glances. Where before the caravan had readily taken over, falling back on old habits and skills, glazing over Terra's inadequacies, now they looked to *her*. Faced with something they'd never imagined, couldn't cope with, they looked to *her*, a washed up office worker. They looked to *her* as a leader.

Can't they see I'm a fraud?

What was Jackson thinking, leaving her in charge? She couldn't do this. She couldn't lead them. She couldn't even save herself. How could she possibly save them?

I'm a hypocrite.

As she continued running her hand through Annie's fine hair, watching the men in black pace back and forth with guns hugged to their shoulders, she had to admit it.

I'm a shifter who's biased against shifters.

God, had she even been able to admit that to herself before? Had she ever managed to say, even in her own head, "I'm a shifter?" She couldn't remember but feared the answer was no. She looked behind herself at the others. A woman whimpered somewhere in the huddle while children hiccupped in anticipation of tears. Fear and trauma stared back at her, serving as the perfect mirror to reflect who she really was.

I'm a monster.

Terra looked around with sad eyes. People shifted on the hard ground as the armed men loomed nearby, their voices indistinct. Her own inner turmoil darkened the situation, leaving her feeling at sea. It's not happy or comfortable to realize you're the bad guy in the plot, that *you're* the one who needs to change, needs to grow, needs to evolve. It was so easy to just assume someone else was in the wrong, that your own problems have outside sources. No one wanted to admit they'd fucked themselves up.

But I let it happen, didn't I?

By listening to the media, the news, by not thinking for herself, by being in denial and not honest with herself, she'd let this happen. Even when Jackson tried to encourage her to learn to shift, she'd refused, burying her head in the sand. Even when Annie started shifting with alacrity, she'd remained in denial. Hell, she'd tried to stop her.

I've got to stop.

She couldn't live in the dark anymore, couldn't hide from her problems and herself a moment longer. Studying her surroundings, something jumped at her.

We outnumber them.

The fact nagged at her consciousness, like a loose stitch on a knit sweater.

We outnumber them.

The bad guys had guns, but *they* had superior numbers. If they could just overpower them, they could get free.

But how? She was no military mastermind, had never been in a fight in her life, and knew her own abilities about as well as a toddler learning its first steps. She struggled to piece together what she knew about shifters, about the skill sets of those who'd stayed behind, and came up blank.

God, I am *a fraud.*

But an urgency was building in her. They needed to *do* something. They needed to act. They couldn't wait around, hoping for a rescue, hoping for a hero. This was the real world, and the real world didn't work that way.

God helps those who help themselves.

And Terra was done letting someone else act for her.

CHAPTER TWENTY-SEVEN

*T*erra sidled up to one of the older women, continuing to hold Annie in her lap. She glanced over to where the armed assailants stood. Maybe a half hour ago, they'd drifted off, convening in small groups around the huddled captives, just out of earshot of normal hearing.

Of course, they were shifters and "just out of normal hearing" didn't mean jack shit. Not that she was listening. She had other plans in mind.

She slid over until her outer thigh bumped up against the woman's. "We need to act." Her voice didn't raise above a whisper and she didn't look at her. She'd chosen her to speak to first because she didn't know who she could rely on. She needed someone who knew the others, knew what they were capable of.

"What do you suggest?" the woman said, her voice trembling from nerves and age.

"Not sure yet. Need to rally the forces first, figure out what we've got."

The woman nodded.

"Most of the fighters left with Jackson." Her voice started to smooth out as she spoke, confidence and purpose easing her. "We don't have much in the way of weapons. Maybe a knife or two."

Terra frowned but tried to mask the expression as soon as it formed. It wouldn't do to give away the game before they even got started. She studied the nearest cluster of armed men. They stood in a loose group. One smoked, a plume billowing into the sky as he sucked hard, the end flaring bright red. None looked this way.

She turned back to her partner in crime. "We outnumber them. Do you think we can take them without weapons?" She glanced over at the woman again, who frowned.

"I want to say yes, but I just don't know. If everyone was here, I would say absolutely. Philippe alone would have been a wonderful asset. He often shifts into a bear and has fought in many wars he felt had merit. But with those here? I just don't know."

Terra bit her lip, chewing on it with worry. Then, Annie tipped her head up, an adorable confused look on her face. "I'll fight, Tewa. I have claws!" She lifted and curled her hands, looking adorably fierce.

A grin curved her lips before she froze.

I have claws.

Every last one of them was a shifter. They could shift into animals with built in weapons. Claws, talons, fangs, you name it.

A plan began to form in her mind.

Terra sat back, her nerves wound tighter than a tourniquet. Before her, two foot tall Timmy was ready to initiate the plan. As she looked around, her team was just as tense, primed for action. It had taken time to organize everyone, maybe an hour in the seemingly unending crawl of captivity, but they were ready now. Everyone knew their parts.

I can't believe I'm using a robot in this plan. This is crazy.

Yet, this was the best she could come up with. She wasn't a tactician. She wasn't a soldier or leader. Give her some paper-work and she could take it on like a boss, but give her a life or death situation and she was hopeless.

Timmy sidled up to the nearest throng of baddies. He proceeded forward on his little legs, wobbling on parts not made for their final purpose. When he stopped, he looked up, focusing on one of the armed men. His simulated voice broke the silence. "You should cup the butt of your rifle to your shoulder to minimize probability of musculoskeletal damage."

"What the fuck?" he said, backing up and staring down at Timmy. "What the fuck is this?"

Another laughed, pointing at the man in question. "Man, that little bucket of bolts *owned* you."

More masculine laughter welled up, all directed at Timmy's target.

"Shut up," he said, pulling his weapon tighter to his shoulder, though, noticeably, doing exactly as Timmy instructed.

"Did the wittle wobot teach you to hold your wittle gun?"

"Shut. Up. Asswipe."

"Hey!" a voice barked from the opposite end of the clearing. "Knock it off." He marched across the space, his steps pounding the dirt.

Terra pivoted her head, monitoring the other men. They started shifting toward the spectacle, helpless to resist the ass chewing about to go down. She turned to her partners in crime and nodded.

The huddle erupted into fur and sharp claws, surging outward seemingly in all directions. Moments later, gunshots cracked through the air. Terra tried to shift as blood splattered the ground around her, but she couldn't focus, couldn't visualize anything in that moment.

She stood there, paralyzed and worthless, as the others struck, attacking with determination. Long, thick limbs swiped out, hitting men so hard they collapsed. To her left, an enormous cat pounced, knocking a man onto his back.

Come on, just shift. Anything.

She stared down at her hands, willing them to *do* something, but her mind was blank. Then a single image popped into her brain, the only time she'd ever really shifted, and her hands changed, forming those digging claws she'd made when she escaped.

Good enough.

She raced forward, coming up behind a man who was being corralled by a large wolf. Pulling back her arm, she walloped him, the dull claws scraping against his back, leaving deep furrows. He screamed, whirling around, but then the wolf pounced, ending him with a rending bite.

Terra turned, looking for another target.

"Enough," that same authoritative voice snapped.

Her gaze zeroed in on the voice, and she froze. He stood in the middle of the fray. Bodies thrashed around him, but he remained still, holding a small, squirming body in one arm as another held a gun to her head.

"Annie!"

CHAPTER TWENTY-EIGHT

*T*erra dropped her hands to her sides, frozen by terror as Annie continued to squirm in the monster's grip.

"Let me *go!*" Annie shrieked as she ground her little nails into his arm and wiggled like she intended to squeeze out above the confining limb.

Around her, the fighting died down, shifters on four legs retreated, sidling up behind Terra, showing a constancy and loyalty she didn't deserve. Someone whined, the animalistic sound making her want to pet the person, soothe them. She didn't dare move a muscle, afraid what the man might do next.

"That's better," he said, ignoring Annie's struggles. "Men?"

With an alarming speed and coordination, the armed men raised their weapons, training them on the shifters. The sharp double click of a dozen guns cocking at once split the air, making her jerk in place.

My God, we're gonna die.

She wanted to close her eyes tight, wait for the end, but Annie was staring at her, pleading silently. She couldn't abandon her.

Then, over the man's shoulder, she spotted movement. Terra blinked, not understanding what she was seeing. She wanted to squint and crane her neck to get a better look, but resisted. She refused to give herself away if it was help arriving.

Although, who could possibly be showing up to help? They were far from civilization. Nobody came out here. It wasn't like a hero would just pop in and check on them.

It could be Jackson, the others, returning.

Her breath seized, that hope surging like an unbearable pressure, obliterating her. It *could* be Jackson. Hadn't they been wondering when the others would return? The battle was over, at least the one to save Earth. Unfortunately, another battle loomed ahead of them. She glared at the man holding Annie, but it didn't even faze him.

Without moving her head, she took in her surroundings, trying to see those around her, trying to form a plan. She still couldn't tell if she'd imagined the movement in the woods. Hell, it could have been a deer for all she knew.

We're on our own here.

Terra had to believe that. She couldn't wait on a rescuer, a hero, to save them. She had to act, but how? What? As she focused back on Annie, that tightness in her chest grew, choking her.

I can't fail. I just can't.

Then, over the bastard's right shoulder, Jackson stepped out of the trees. Relief surged through her, grateful to not be alone. But he was over there, too far away to make a difference. Around him, more people in camo slipped from the trees and underbrush, forming a thick line.

Wait. She mouthed the word at Jackson and he froze, holding an arm up to stop the others. They dropped into a crouch, pulling their weapons in tighter, ready on her signal.

A weird calm settled over her as she first looked at Annie, her beautiful precocious Annie, then at the enemy leader who continued barking orders as Terra's mind wandered off, forming a plan.

She stared him down, not afraid, as the plan solidified in her mind.

You might be in danger.

Jackson had received that call just a few hours ago. He didn't know the man, had never met him, but something about his tone had resonated with him from the first moment he answered the phone.

He'd hoped Kyle Avery was wrong, that his hunch was unfounded, but as they drove to the caravan's site, they passed big black SUVs lined up along the dirt road. Jackson's hands had flexed against his steering wheel when he'd spotted them.

Those shouldn't be here.

They were in the middle of nowhere, far from popular sites to get lost in nature, and those three big SUVs could easily carry eight people a piece. He'd driven past, craning his neck to see, but his stomach sank, churning away with anxiety.

Are they okay?

He didn't even want to think about it, instead turning to face ahead, toward what they would be facing. As many as two dozen mercenaries could be at the caravan *this* instant, threatening his people, Annie, *Terra*.

His heart seized in his chest, and for a moment, he had trouble breathing.

Dear God, no.

He drove at recklessly fast speeds down the rutted road, his head smacking a time or two against the ceiling when he hit a rut too hard. The entire time, he reminded himself his caravan could take care of themselves.

Except for Terra.

The thought latched on just as he started to convince himself that everything would be all right. Unfortunately, Terra could barely shift, had only done it a couple times, knew nothing about weapons or fighting. She was smart, resourceful, and strong, but she was no fighter.

He hit another rut with a thunk of the suspension as the SUV bottomed out, smacking into the ground, and slowed. They were getting too close. If there *was* a danger, they couldn't afford to let on that they approached.

He pulled over and waited, checking the rearview mirror as more vehicles stopped, and people disembarked. He spotted Philippe's pickup truck and the military transport truck stopping behind him, then opened his door, stepping down on the hard, dusty road.

To his left, rocks skittered across the lane as people and cars disturbed them. Philippe and Avery closed the distance, stopping in silence. He waited for direction. This was Avery's show, the military officer stiff and silent as dry fall leaves rustled and fell around them.

Minutes passed, and their entire group closed in, a tense anticipation thrumming through them.

Avery nodded and finally spoke. "The site is at the end of this lane?" He pointed down the road, asking Jackson.

"Yes. Less than a mile."

"We continue in silence. You know the terrain best. What is your suggestion?"

Jackson frowned. "We should follow the path until shortly before it opens up onto the caravan site. It takes a sharp curve right before that, which will keep us obscured until then."

"Not travel through the trees and underbrush?"

Jackson shook his head. "We should avoid that as much as possible. There are too many dry leaves. It would be difficult to go unheard."

Avery agreed, and Jackson wondered what type of assignments he'd run in the past if that hadn't occurred to him. "We stop just within the tree line. Do *not* be seen. I'll evaluate the situation and direct you accordingly."

Around him, mumbled voices and movements telegraphed everyone's assent and they took off, letting Jackson lead once more. Philippe slipped in beside him, speaking in a whisper. "Do you think Macey and Beth are okay?"

Jackson almost stopped in place, his steps losing their steady rhythm at his friend's question. He couldn't honestly say. He'd paid little attention to the two since they'd arrived at the caravan, only really noticing how much Philippe seemed enamored of them. His mind had been filled with Terra and Annie, but Philippe's charges, hell any of those they'd rescued from the shifter camp, were even more vulnerable.

It was unlikely any of them had ever shifted before. For all intents and purposes, they were human, with human sensibilities and faults. Like humans, they'd grown soft, forgetting the very survival instincts and skills that would have helped them now. He didn't want to tell his friend that, though. Philippe was already worried. Jackson didn't need to add to it.

Before long, he spotted the curve in the road and slipped off the path, edging around wild bushes and underbrush. Despite his best efforts, leaves crackled under his feet and he winced, but continued onward. He advanced, watching his feet, but had to jerk his head up constantly to make sure he didn't walk into an ambush or something.

Wouldn't that *be just my luck?*

Finally, he stopped and crouched at the edge of the forest, staring out from behind an especially dense thicket. He wanted to curse. A group of men in black with guns poised stood with their backs to them. In front of the guns, the people they'd left behind waited to die, some in human and some in animal forms.

Avery came up to his side. "Damn, they're shifters, aren't they?"

Jackson glanced over his shoulder at the whispered comment. "Yes."

"It just... never occurred to me. Mila's only ever shifted parts of herself before. Remarkable."

Jackson ignored the comment. He knew damn well Mila had fully shifted. So did Avery, if he knew her. He gathered she'd been living in another person's skin for a time. "Strategy?"

Avery craned his head, looking off to the side. "Wait until everyone's in position and sneak up behind them."

"That's a lot of distance."

"My men can make it, can yours?" Avery smirked, a challenge in his eyes.

Jackson didn't dignify it with a response.

Moments passed, then Avery signaled, and they surged forward, stepping out into the open. Immediately, he spot-

219

ted Terra. She stood stiff, tension pulsing through her form. Then her gaze locked on his, and her mouth moved, forming a single word.

Wait.

Jackson slapped an arm out, holding Avery back. The man glared at him, but motioned the others to stop too. Avery stared him down accusingly, but Jackson didn't know how to explain. He didn't understand himself. He looked back at Terra. She appeared frozen solid, but the longer he watched, the more her face transformed, a plan forming.

What is she up to?

Terra stared down at Annie, ignoring Jackson and the line of men forming at the tree line. She knew what she had to do, what *they* had to do.

This will work. It has to.

"Shift," she whispered.

Annie froze in the man's grip, not reacting for a moment. Terra nodded, giving her permission for the first time.

And hopefully not the last.

Annie smiled, then shifted into a cougar, her little voice crying out in a sound that was a mix between a sheep and a bird chirping. The man jumped, losing his grip on the little wildcat who quickly dropped to the ground on all fours and dashed behind Terra, losing herself in the group of shifters.

Terra pounced, not even thinking as she leapt at the cold-hearted bastard who would use a toddler as a shield. For the first time, the shift came effortlessly to her. She didn't have to imagine something in her head. She didn't have to focus. Her body *knew* what to do and took over, ready to protect her little girl.

She slammed into his body with full force as he screamed. They crashed to the ground with a jarring thud, and she screamed in his face, though the sound didn't register. He froze, eyes wide, not even breathing as movement blurred in her periphery.

———

Jackson looked over at Avery, who stood tense as if a single thread held him in place. When Terra pounced, turning into a cougar and tackling one of the men in black, they didn't need a command. They acted.

Startled by Terra's transformation, Jackson fell behind a few steps as the others surged forward to join the fight.

She shifted.

He couldn't believe it. With all the times he'd tried to get her to shift, she'd finally done it.

She shifted.

He shook himself, noticing his allies racing across the empty distance, and rushed forward at full speed, trying to catch up. They spread out, forming a solid line behind the threat, as the people they'd left behind took Terra's attack as a rallying cry, her wild screams piercing the air.

Though he had a gun strapped across his body, he didn't use it, not with innocents in the line of fire. As he surged up behind a black-clad body, he let a wicked cross loose, spinning the man around, lining him up for a perfect shot to the throat. He went down in a sprawl of limbs as predators attacked all around him, swiping with paws or biting down with strong jaws to subdue.

He tipped his head up, searching for Terra. Standing on four legs, she'd abandoned her unconscious foe as she spun around, chirping for all she was worth. The high pitched, almost birdlike sound, made him smile, until he realized she was looking for Annie.

Jackson stepped up to Terra, adding his eyes to the search, but didn't see the little girl he'd come to know and love anywhere on the battlefield.

And it *was* a battlefield. Though few gunshots burst through the air, blood and death littered the ground as clashes of bodies surrounded him.

Where is she?

He wanted to call out to her, but he held the words in, afraid of drawing attention to their search.

Terra chirped again and dashed forward, Jackson on her heels. She cuddled around a small cougar and Jackson smiled, then took his gun off his shoulder, using it as a blunt weapon to protect his family.

A body bumped against the back of his lower leg and he looked behind him, finding Terra covering his back, swiping at anyone who came near. Annie hid mostly underneath her, chirping adorably at each person who approached.

It didn't take long before the fight ended, leaving military and shifters the only ones standing. Some of the enemy lay on the ground unconscious while others sat huddled, cornered by his allies.

Avery barked out orders as the bad guys were secured. Someone ran off for the tree line in the direction they'd left the vehicles. Jackson stared at Terra and Annie and smiled, kneeling down to their level. Annie pounced on his lap, chirping at him happily, while Terra leaned into him, likewise happy to see him. He pulled them close, digging his fingers deep into their furs, relieved to find them both safe and unharmed.

After the fight, the caravan had slipped off to the periphery. Some were shaken, keeping out in the open where they could see a new threat coming. Others just wanted the familiarity of home and disappeared into their respective trailers. Those they'd rescued from the shifter camp seemed mostly unnerved, skittish. They watched the soldiers with skepticism and fear, but they had nowhere to go, so many of them huddled together, taking comfort in each other.

Jackson had retreated with Terra, Annie, Philippe, Macey, and Beth to the space in front of Philippe's trailer. The group gathered around a small bonfire that just pushed back the sharp, chill air that spoke of the winter yet to come. The flames crackled, little sparks dancing in the air around them.

Terra and Annie remained in cougar form. Annie bounced around the fire, occasionally staying put just long enough to get a few pets before bounding off again. Beth looked after her with yearning.

Terra lay next to Jackson, but facing the area where Avery still interrogated the men they'd captured. At least, he did with the conscious ones. He'd ordered the unconscious ones to the transport truck they'd pulled up into the clearing. Now, a couple men guarded it in case the captives awoke. Her tail twitched back and forth, her body a tense spring of silent menace. He kept a hand on her neck and shoulders, reminding her of his presence.

Or maybe holding her back.

When Avery waved the last of the prisoners to the truck,

Jackson stood, patting Terra on the back. He'd hoped she would stay behind, but she rose to her feet, following beside him like a dog heeling. He walked up to Avery and reached out his hand. "Thank you."

Avery took it, shaking it with a palm rough with grit. "Any time."

"What now?" he asked as Avery released him.

The military officer smirked. "Now I round them up."

Jackson frowned.

What did that mean?

CHAPTER TWENTY-NINE

K yle walked into a swanky office building, pushing the swinging glass doors before him as a team of men followed behind him, ready to do his bidding. He didn't foresee a challenge here, but the building was high profile. Then again, so was the entire damned case. They needed a win, desperately.

And nothing spelled victory like a corporate suit being frog marched out of his own headquarters by a half dozen badasses in uniform.

He didn't bother with the front desk. In full-blown misogyny, a woman in a low-cut blouse stood from her seat, squawking as he ignored her to head for the elevators.

"Hey! You're supposed to sign in first."

He walked to the first elevator, pressing the metal "Up" button, and stepped back to wait. His team filled the lobby around the bank of elevators, leaving the few people passing through or stopping to take an elevator uneasy. They stood at parade rest with pistols at their hips, a stark contrast to the rest of the people flowing through the area. They were like a mountain surrounded by running water. Unmovable. Unstoppable.

The elevator dinged, and they slipped in together. The space was large, but they barely fit. Kyle pressed the button for the top floor and smirked.

He waited impatiently with his hands pulled behind his back as the car rose, dragging down on his body with each foot. When it dinged again, he stepped out, moving to the right without even glancing at the open central floor plan flanked by offices. He continued onward as people in fancy suits, mostly men, glanced at him, alarmed.

He stopped at the last office, which had smoky glass double doors and white lettering etched onto the glass reading, "Stewart Xavier, CEO."

Avery pushed the doors open, revealing a secretary on the phone. Another woman in a low-cut shirt, her mouth hung open. The phone drifted away from her ear as she sat there. He ignored her and rounded her desk, aiming for the door behind her.

"Hey, you can't go in there," she said in a high-pitched voice.

He grabbed the door handle and pushed it open, stepping into the enormous office. Behind the desk, a man in a shiny suit stopped in mid-action, then put his phone down and knitted his hands together. "Can I help you?" he asked, his tone acidic.

"Stewart Xavier, you are under arrest." Kyle pulled out the card from his back pocket, a card that had "Miranda Rights" on one side and "Article 31b Rights" on the other. He didn't usually arrest civilians, so he didn't have these rights memorized. "You have the right to remain silent. Anything you say can and will be used against you in a court of law. You have the right to an attorney. If you cannot afford an attorney, one will be provided for you. You can decide at any time from this moment on to exercise these rights. Do you understand each of these rights I have explained to you?"

Mila slipped into the hospital room, a tote bag pulled tight to her side. As the door closed with a hiss, she half expected a nurse to come charging in to confiscate her bounty. When nothing happened, she sighed and crossed the room, dropping onto the edge of Tristan's bed. The bag landed in his lap.

"What's this?"

"Fuel," she said with a smirk.

He peeled open the canvas, hamburger and fry fumes bursting out. "Thanks." He dug in, starting with the burger.

The room quieted as he ate, conversation replaced by a TV reporter reporting the news. "In national news, the National Space Service arrested individuals from the terrorist organization, MEGA." Mila turned around, the mention of the NSS catching her attention. "MEGA, short for Make Earth Great Again, was responsible for sabotage and attacks on the Incirrina Treaty missions. It is also implicated in a group of attacks on shape-shifters throughout the United States."

On screen, Avery and a half dozen MPs walked out of a set of glass doors, dragging a man in a fancy suit to their vehicle. The prisoner appeared outraged, puffed up with his own superiority complex. Behind him, Avery looked confident and proud.

"Good for him."

Tristan swallowed hard beside her. "Oh?"

She pointed at the screen. "Avery finally got his man."

Mila stood against the backdrop, trying to keep a straight face. It was hard to stay stoic when she just wanted to grin from ear to ear, but she didn't want the tech to have to take the photograph again. The camera flashed, and she blinked, splotches of color blinding her for a few moments.

With a nod, the person led her to a workstation at the RAPIDS site. "Place your hand on the panel."

She did, and after a few clicks from him, the panel lit up like a flatbed scanner. "Ow." She resisted the urge to pull away from the pinching stab to her fingertip.

"That's the genetic ID sample," he said, not looking up from his display.

Mila sat, squirming in her seat. She didn't have the patience of Job, even under the best of circumstances. Here, she was on the cusp, a tipping point in her life, and she couldn't wait.

A machine hummed in the background, and the man got up. He returned with a small rectangle in hand. Mila leaned forward, subconsciously reaching for it even if her hands stayed in her lap.

"Here you go," he said, handing it over.

Mila looked down, strong emotion choking her. "Thanks." She stood up, not able to take her eyes off the little bit of plastic.

A verified ID.

Her eyes teared up as she moved toward the door. She ducked her head, but otherwise did nothing to hide her emotion.

"Pilot Dragomirov?" someone called from behind her.

She turned around, blinking away the moisture, her new Common Access Card clutched to her chest. "Yes?"

"I have a couple messages for you. They're to be hand delivered."

Mila reached out, taking the two envelopes. "Thanks."

He saluted, then about-faced and left.

Mila was torn. She didn't have enough hands to hold the ID and check the contents of the envelopes. It took all of a moment for her to shove her ID in her pocket and open the first one. Her mouth dropped. A federal pardon for impersonating a member of the military. When the Commandant had confronted her about her identity, she'd been terrified, and as a huge weight lifted off her shoulders, she realized she'd still been worried. But she needn't worry any longer. She sighed, all her muscles relaxing at once.

Next, she opened the other envelope. Inside was an invitation to a formal Medal of Honor ceremony to be held in D.C. For her. She clutched it to her chest, shaking her head, a little smile on her face. Sure, the President had said he would, but that was a press conference. That could have easily been posturing. This was real.

She still couldn't believe it, though. Walking out of the building, she stared at it, trying to process the news. She'd expected her stint in the military would be limited, a brief bout of happiness before she lost it all again. She'd wanted to grasp as much of the experience as she could, make the most of every moment. Mila never expected *this*.

CHAPTER THIRTY

ila waited in her living room, pacing erratically as she rubbed her sweaty palms on her pants. Tristan sat on the couch, cool as can be. She growled at him. "Why are you so calm?"

He shrugged. "Because we'll get through this. We can get through anything." He smirked, taking the edge, the intensity, off the statement. He'd just been released from the hospital earlier that day. His movements were still a bit stiff, but he insisted he was fine. She didn't quite believe him.

They're coming.

The thought slipped into her head, and her anxiety ratcheted up again. She couldn't do this. She wasn't ready, but would she ever be?

I hope so.

The doorbell rang, and she jumped, turning to the open doorway.

Tristan got up with a wince and touched her shoulder, the small gesture calming her slightly. "I'll get it."

Mila held her breath, lost in that moment. She'd agonized over how to handle this. What face should she show them? What would be the least shocking? May's face? Mila's face? She'd been on TV, but maybe they'd missed it. Maybe they hadn't seen.

It had been Tristan who suggested her current course of action. She stood in jeans and a blouse, uncomfortable in the casual attire. She wanted to be in uniform, wearing that armor to protect herself. Maybe she could go get changed? Her uniform spoke to who she was: pilot, soldier, Dragomirov.

No, someone was already here. Of course, she couldn't change.

Change. She scoffed. The irony. She would change all right.

May's parents walked through the door, a little puzzled.

"May, what's going on? Why are you so nervous?" May's mother said, walking up and rubbing her upper arms, trying to soothe her. The gentle look in the other woman's eyes nearly broke her.

She couldn't do it. She couldn't take the woman's daughter away from her.

But this was a lie. They deserved to know.

"Have you seen Mila? Talked to her?" May's father said, touching his hands to his wife's shoulders, providing that strength and support.

"Yeah, I have."

"Is that what this is about?" the other woman said.

Mila sniffed, whispering, "Yeah," under her breath

The doorbell rang again and Tristan, standing in the living room doorway, slipped out gingerly to answer it.

Moments later, Mila's parents walked through the door. Mila's eyes watered, but she held herself back. Did her father know? Did her mother tell him? She'd asked them here because she needed everything in the open, but also because her mom had always been friends with Mrs. Trace. She'd hoped her presence would soften the blow.

"May, are you all right?" her mother said, voice rising with alarm and concern.

"I have something to tell you guys."

Alyana looked into her daughter's eyes, and just like when she figured out Mila had been masquerading as May, she figured this out too. She saw her daughter's difficulty and relaxed, voicing the words that lodged in Mila's throat like a rock. "You're Mila," she said, confident and calm.

"What?!" May's mother squawked, her head rotating between Mila and her mother. "No, she's…" But she stopped, pain crossing her face.

Alyana went up to her friend, hugging her tight. "You knew. Deep down, you knew just as I did."

Mrs. Trace nodded against her friend's shoulder. "I didn't want… I couldn't admit…"

"I know, I know." Her mom turned to her. "What happened?"

Mila paused, unsure what she wanted to know, so she changed forms, unable to bear the pain wearing May's face was causing the couple in front of her. She spilled it all. She told them about shape-shifting for the first time, about running away. She told them about meeting up with May after ten years, about the mugging, the *Orleans*, everything. At times, May's mother gripped her friend tighter, emotion getting the better of her, but they kept quiet, let her finish.

Moments passed in silence after she finished speaking. She

looked at them, trying to read their emotions, their thoughts from their faces, their body language. Not that she was any good at that.

After a while, they settled, pulling away from each other, and Mila realized that Tristan had come up behind her, reaching his arms around her middle. She lifted her hands, clutching his as both sets of parents turned to her and Tristan.

Mila gnawed at her lip, afraid of what they would say. Would they condemn her? Hate her for her lie? For not giving them the opportunity to grieve?

May's mother sniffed, rubbing a finger under each eye. "You've always been like a daughter to us." She shook her head. "I never imagined. It must have been awful."

"We can have May properly buried," Mila blurted out, not being able to take the kindness, the acceptance.

But the other woman only nodded, then came up to Mila and hugged her.

Mila stood outside the East Room of the White House in her dress uniform. She felt exposed, even more so than when she'd participated in the press conference. At least the press conference a week ago hadn't just been about her. This *was*.

"Breathe," the President said beside her. "Just breathe."

She sucked in a huge breath, the influx of oxygen settling her nerves. "Thanks."

He nodded. "Are you ready?"

No, but it didn't matter. She still couldn't believe she'd spent the last hour in the Oval office talking to the President in casual conversation. They'd chatted about her life, about what she'd been through. He never once judged her, not for any of it. She didn't vote for him, but if he were up for election, she would. He was a good man.

Music swelled from the room before them, and the door opened.

An announcer said, "Ladies and Gentlemen, the President of the United States accompanied by Medal of Honor recipient Pilot Mila Anya Dragomirov."

The President nodded, and Mila started walking. All around her, people held up cell phones, taking pictures and videos as she and the President passed through the middle of the crowd. With each step, having such a powerful, important man behind her made her want to run, triggering long outdated survival instincts.

They moved to the front of the room where a dais took center stage. They faced the audience, the President on her left. She stood at attention, hands behind her back, using that stance, that familiarity, to give her strength.

Before her, her family and friends sat in the first and second row. Tristan, Mila's parents, May's parents, Kyle Avery, and even Luke Hall and Jackson. She took strength from them being here as well.

The music ended, and a man in uniform walked up to a podium to her left. "Let us pray.

"Almighty God, today we honor an American soldier deserving of our nation's highest respect. She deserves this admiration for the bravery, valor, and heroism she has displayed…"

Mila tried not to listen, growing increasingly uncomfortable with all the grandstanding and the sincerity with which he spoke her praise. She wasn't used to it, and she didn't like it. She just wanted to run and hide, forget this ever happened.

The man finished his prayer with an "amen" then the President stepped forward, started talking. "We all know of the terrible events that lead to this day. The whole world was made aware in those hours of our vulnerability to threats that we, as a whole, never once speculated on. But it is because of men and women like Pilot Mila Dragomirov that we can continue to speculate, even plan, for our future.

"Because of her, we won that fight, can keep fighting. Because of her, more good soldiers were not lost. We can not honor her enough for the risks she took, the dangers she faced. We thank you." He turned to her, bowing his head.

"I would like to welcome Mila's family and friends, many of whom she's served with. I want to also thank and honor Pilot May Trace, who discovered a plot to sabotage the USS *Orleans* and, not knowing who to turn to, reached out to a friend, thus starting Mila on this path and changing hers and our lives forever.

"I would like to welcome the members of the Medal of Honor Society," he nodded at a group of current and former soldiers to the left who wore their medals around their necks, "who are welcoming their sister soldier into their ranks today. We are very proud of all who have served so gallantly."

He turned back to Mila, smiling. "When I first met Mila, I had no idea the depths to her character or struggle. When I talked with her, she often said things like, 'I didn't want this,' or 'I don't deserve this.' She insisted anyone would have done the same. By then, I already knew about her past, about how great a risk she'd taken as she served.

"Mila, as a shifter hiding among the military, could have lost her freedom at any time, yet she never let that stop her, risking her life on board the USS *Orleans* to save her crew even though she didn't have the training. She refused to leave her fate and the fate of the entire crew in others' hands.

"She ran ahead and fought off a half dozen men so her team would have time to suit up, to survive when the airlock was opened, so they could close the hatch and save the rest of the crew. Sucked into space, she nearly made the ultimate sacrifice for that difficult decision.

"At the Kennedy Moon Station, she was involved in the early warning required to coordinate forces, taking off even though the enemy ship could have shot them out of the sky.

"On Earth, she was the one who suggested and coordinated the alliance with the shape-shifter community, a move that could also have led to loss of her freedom, a freedom she had exercised when she ran away ten years ago, risking a life on the streets rather than one in the shifter camps.

"Now, if the military aide would please come forward."

Two men stepped into place. One held a warm wood case with a glass window in front of his abdomen as he faced the crowd, standing to the left of the President. The other went to a podium behind them. "The President of the United States of America, authorized by Act of Congress, March 3, 1863, has awarded in the name of Congress the Medal of Honor to Pilot Mila Anya Dragomirov, National Space Service, for conspicuous gallantry and intrepidity at the risk of life and liberty above and beyond the call of duty."

He continued on, repeating much of what the President had already said. After a spell, he became quiet and the man to her left handed the medal to the President, who then posed with her for a picture. Applause rang through the room as everyone stood. Mila smiled down at Tristan, who gave her an ear to ear grin.

"Thank you all who have served, as members of the military or not. Thank you, Mila. God bless you. God bless America."

The room broke out in applause once more, and Mila turned to the people that mattered most, not wanting the praise, and certainly not needing it.

Terra stood in her old apartment, feeling a little shellshocked. She still couldn't believe she was doing this.

I'm saying goodbye.

Most of her apartment was now in boxes or had been donated. Annie gamboled around, giggling and playing a game only *she* could fathom. Terra's heart constricted in her chest. They'd been trying to find Annie's parents but no luck so far. She honestly couldn't decide if she hoped to find them or not. She loved Annie and couldn't bear to lose her. And yet, what about Annie's parents? Were they now pining away for the child they'd lost?

Unfortunately, things were still risky for her kind. The Shifter Rights and Identification Act had just been proposed in Congress and while it was a step forward, until it passed, her place in society was tenuous at best. The President had promptly shut down the shifter camps, released the captives, and promised restitution, but that didn't stop prejudice or discrimination. It didn't stop people from thinking of her and the rest of the shifter community as subhuman. It didn't protect them from being singled out.

A chill ran up her spine, and she suddenly just wanted to return to the caravan. They'd decided to wait, again, to move to the new site so she could close out her old life. Also because Mila had invited Jackson to her friend, May's, funeral. Terra never met the woman who'd passed, but she suspected Jackson needed outside perspectives, so she'd encouraged him to go, feeling that fostering a friendship with the military pilot would be good for him.

"All done?" he asked, coming up behind her.

She faced him and smiled. "Looks like it." She turned back to the boxes. It was still quite a lot, and Jackson's trailer was tiny. "Where are we going to put all this?"

"Don't worry about it. We'll figure it out."

She shook her head. "None of this stuff matters."

"It's yours. Thus it matters."

"I could leave all this behind and be completely happy. I just want to go home."

He beamed at her. "Home, huh?"

"Yeah."

He leaned in, a mischievous glint emerging in his eyes. "Well, just for that, I'm going to teach you a new trick when we get 'home'."

She grinned ear to ear, her body thrumming with excitement. "Really?"

"Oh yes."

She laughed. "I can't wait."

Kyle pulled at his collar. He never met May Trace in life and couldn't see how attending her wake made any sense, but Mila had invited him, almost begging him to come, so he stood at the back, wondering when it would be over. The wake hadn't officially started, so people milled around, drinking and munching on cookies. He let the sea of people wash over him, the din of overlapping voices nothing but white noise.

Before long, people started wandering to folding chairs set up in rows in the middle of the room. Kyle sat down and spotted Mila and Tristan entering through a side door, hands clasped together. He smiled, then they spotted him and made a path through the crowd, aiming straight at him.

He tensed.

"Avery, I'm glad you made it," Mila said, smiling at him. The smile didn't quite reach her eyes, speaking to the conflicted emotions she still dealt with.

He shrugged, not knowing what to say. What *did* you say to a woman who stole the decedent's identity and buried her in the woods?

She touched his arm, gaining his attention once more. "I was hoping you might say a few words?"

"What? I didn't know her."

"Yeah, but we were all touched by her in some way."

He frowned, but nodded. She needed the support. So be it.

"Thanks." She patted him again and dragged Tristan up to the front by his hand.

A few moments later, a male voice spoke up. "Well, I didn't expect to see *you* here."

He spun around, spotting Shandor Jackson, the shifter targeted by MEGA. "Or you."

Jackson shrugged, the action lifting his woman's arm by their joined hands. "Mila invited me."

Kyle looked around. "Did she invite everyone?"

Jackson chuckled. "I have no idea."

The two sat next to him. The woman reached over Jackson, offering Kyle her hand. "I'm Terra, by the way."

"Kyle." Her grip was surprisingly firm as they shook hands. "Did you know her?"

"No," she shook her head. "Just showing support. I did meet Mila, though."

He nodded. "I think we all have."

Up ahead, a man in black stood at a podium next to the closed casket. Clearing his voice, the room quieted, and the stragglers settled in their seats. "We are here to honor the life of May Trace, pilot in the National Space Service, and beloved daughter and friend."

Kyle tuned out as the officiant began a prayer. Before long, the man stepped down, disappearing off to the side as a middle-aged couple stepped up with tears in their eyes. May's parents. They spoke of her as a child, of her dreams and fantasies, of her skills. They talked of her friends, especially Mila. After a few minutes, the mother broke into tears and the two returned to their seats, settling into the first row where another woman hugged her and rocked her back and forth.

A few more people talked about May's life before Mila approached the podium. Her eyes looked glassy with her tears, her voice thick with emotion. "May was my best friend, my twin, my other half. We did everything together." She shook her head as emotion built, choking her. "She died doing what was right. I'm sorry. I can't."

She dashed back down to the front row and nobody said anything, understanding entirely. Then Kyle's name was called, and he stood, walking down a central aisle. When he reached the podium, he looked down at the others and froze.

I shouldn't be here.

Any one of these people could have spoken to May's life better than him. He didn't know her, had never met her. What could he possibly say to honor her life?

His hands gripped the worn wood as he took a deep breath. "I never met May Trace, not the real one. The first time I saw who I thought was May Trace, I knew something was off about her. Not a threat, but not honest either. I guess, deep down, I always knew that woman was a shifter in disguise, Mila." He held out his hand at Mila in the audience.

"What I do know about her is that she was a mediocre pilot, but in spite of that, she never gave up. She never quit, even when her friend disappeared." He felt grateful for the research he'd done into May Trace before he'd known she was a shifter. It was coming in handy now. "She lived her life serving this country with integrity. This is what got her killed, but never forget that. As far as I'm concerned, she was just as deserving of the Medal of Honor as Mila Dragomirov was. She not only identified a possible threat, she took measures to record it, documenting evidence that would later serve vital. When she didn't know who to trust, she didn't freeze up and bury what she knew, figuring she couldn't do anything about it. No, she went outside the system, going to someone she *could* trust for advice.

"May Trace died a hero, trying to protect this country." He saluted her. "And with her actions, she brought people together, creating alliances that have served to protect the *world*. I salute you, May Trace. Thank you."

241

GET AN EXCLUSIVE NOVELLA

I love building relationships with my readers. As part of that, I regularly send emails with deleted scenes, never before seen excerpts, pre-order and new release announcements, and more.

If you sign up to receive these emails, I'll send you <u>Mila's Flight</u>, the prequel to the Darkest Day series, FREE.

Join Now to Get Your Free Ebook

www.theeternalscribe.com

DID YOU ENJOY THE BOOK?

If so, you can make a BIG difference...

Reviews are among the most important tools in my arsenal for getting my books in front of readers like yourself. I'm just one person. No matter how much I shout, my voice can only carry so far.

But do you want to know what does carry?

A crowd.

When one voice joins another who joins another, that matters. *That* gets heard.

Let your own voice be heard by leaving an honest review. It only takes a few minutes, but makes a major difference not just to me as an author, but to readers like yourself who are trying to decide on their next read.

Thanks again!

Danielle

ACKNOWLEDGMENTS

A special thanks to the following members of Wattpad for making this book the best it could be. Your comments are always appreciated.

dforrest

ABOUT THE AUTHOR

Danielle Forrest is a Paranormal SciFi author and Medical Laboratory Scientist based out of Indianapolis, IN.

She has dedicated her life so far to two things:

Science & Books

So it really shouldn't be a surprise if science finds its way into even the most fantastical examples of her writing.

Sign up for her mailing list at www.theeternalscribe.com to get access to exclusive content and updates.

facebook.com/theeternalscribe

twitter.com/theeternalscribe

instagram.com/theeternalscribe

goodreads.com/theeternalscribe

amazon.com/author/danielleforrest

bookbub.com/profile/danielle-forrest

ALSO BY DANIELLE FORREST

THE DARKEST DAY SERIES

Mila's Flight

When she shifts for the first time, an unsuspecting shape-shifter runs away to live on the streets. But after a mysterious man enters her life violently, she'll die if she doesn't stop running from her problems.

Mila's Shift

Hiding from a government bent on eradicating her kind, a paranoid shape-shifter steals her dead friend's identity to board a military spaceship, but when the captain discovers her secret, she must learn to trust again or no one will survive.

Tristan's Choice

After he receives orders for a new mission, an unambitious space ship captain transports diplomats to the moon for a historic treaty negotiation with an alien race. But when an alien ship attacks, interrupting the talks, he must warn Earth or everyone will die.

BONUS SCENE

Jackson sat next to Terra, an arm over her shoulders, pulling her close to his side. Annie squirmed next to them, waiting for the announcement. It was expected that the Shifter Rights and Identification Act would be passed today, should have already been passed. Months had gone by since that press conference. Jackson had been the face of shifters to a lot of people ever since, and Terra had nagged him until he made good use of it.

The President had promised that day that he would make changes, but Jackson had never had faith in promises, especially from humans. It was Terra, though, who pushed him to take action, to lobby for changes, alter public opinion, instead of hiding in the shadows hoping the world would pass him by. It hadn't taken much for him to agree.

He smiled, playfully rubbing the top of Annie's head, to which she scowled at him, the look adorable on her youthful face. These two had changed him. For the better, and he was grateful for it. His old self wouldn't have done half the things he'd done recently, and he couldn't help thinking that was tragic.

What had he been doing with his life? He'd lived so long and yet had hidden more than anything, isolating himself and his people when he could have done so much more.

Now, they were back at the caravan site where he'd first welcomed Terra and Annie, and he'd never felt a sense of home like this before. Somehow, it was so much bigger than it had ever been before. They still lived off the land, off their skills, but they didn't fear the outside world as they once did. Surprisingly, Terra had taught him that.

He pulled her closer to his side, reveling in the warmth and companionship. He refocused on the TV. On screen, C-SPAN showed the congressional floor, and the ticker at the bottom changed. "SRIA passed in Senate 66-34."

They were finally safe, protected.

Free.

CPSIA information can be obtained
at www.ICGtesting.com
Printed in the USA
BVHW041604110520
579510BV00003B/182

9 781950 795048